The Lives and Deaths of Matthew St. Clare

Karyn —
I hope you like my novel. It's been great getting to know you, and I wish you joy and good health.
Regards,
Andrew
6/10

The Lives and Deaths of Matthew St. Clare

Andrew Jantz

Copyright © 2009 by Andrew Jantz.

Library of Congress Control Number:		2009913295
ISBN:	Hardcover	978-1-4500-1186-0
	Softcover	978-1-4500-1185-3
	Ebook	978-1-4500-1187-7

All rights reserved. No part of this book may be reproduced or transmitted in any form or by any means, electronic or mechanical, including photocopying, recording, or by any information storage and retrieval system, without permission in writing from the copyright owner.

This is a work of fiction. Names, characters, places and incidents either are the product of the author's imagination or are used fictitiously, and any resemblance to any actual persons, living or dead, events, or locales is entirely coincidental.

This book was printed in the United States of America.

To order additional copies of this book, contact:
Xlibris Corporation
1-888-795-4274
www.Xlibris.com
Orders@Xlibris.com
72271

*For I am ready to fall,
and my pain is ever with me.*

Psalms: 38:17

Prelude

Matthew St. Clare, at age thirty-four, was about to undergo the first in a series of twelve electro-convulsive therapy treatments, popularly known as shock treatments, and he was scared. He'd seen the videos on such "therapy" and how innocuous it is today, compared to the painful, barbaric and mind-erasing treatment depicted in "One Flew Over the Cuckoo's Nest". He'd met with doctors who had assured him he'd be unconscious through the entire process, and that after a full course of treatments he could expect some relief from clinical depression, with perhaps some follow-up sessions—"maintenance" they called it—to keep the depression at bay. But Matthew was nervous anyway, because he'd talked to other patients in the psych ward who'd received ECT, and some of them had tried to talk him out of it. They confirmed that you don't feel anything while you are unconscious, but when you wake up your brain feels scrambled, and more importantly, while you might experience some relief from depression, the effects are usually short-lived, even with follow-ups. Furthermore, large swaths of your memory are often erased, as one might erase a video tape. That is what frightened Matthew the most, for what is a human being without memories? He would lose his identity. The doctors would only admit that memory loss was a possibility, and that most patients have a minimal loss, if any at all. That did not reassure him.

A nurse woke him at 5:30 that first morning, when everyone else in the psych ward was asleep (or tossing and turning, unable to sleep at all). He was still groggy from his nighttime meds. A kindly looking older nurse brought in a wheelchair and asked if he was ready.

"Not really," he said, and frankly told her that he was frightened.

Like a doting grandmother she tried to ease his fears while she inserted a port into the back of his hand, through which the anesthetic would be pumped. Matthew's heart was pounding. She wheeled him through the normally locked doors of the ward, and out to the elevator for the ride to the basement, where the treatments were administered. Several other people in white coats appeared, and helped him onto the bed in the little bay surrounded by a curtain, separating him from the several other patients. Shortly afterward the doctor came and told him to relax, that it was a painless procedure, other than the temporary headache and disorientation he'd feel for a couple of hours afterward. A gel-like paste was smeared onto his temples, and large electrodes pressed into the paste. The anesthesiologist connected an IV bag to the port in his hand, and told him to count backward from 100. He felt a cool liquid flow into his arm. Before he even reached 90, Matthew felt the marvelous cloak of unconsciousness cover him, and he was gone.

When he woke, he felt exactly like they said he'd feel: a throbbing headache, disoriented, and the queer feeling that his brain had been scrambled like eggs. They wheeled him back up to his room, helped him into bed, and left him alone for the rest of the day; i.e., he was excused from all the therapy groups and could just sleep off the effects of the treatment.

And so he did. He finally woke in the late afternoon, and felt better: the headache was mostly gone, and his thoughts felt reasonably ordered again. He was still deeply depressed, but the doctors had told him it would take several, or more, ECT treatments before he really noticed a difference. He did not, however, feel afraid anymore, and in fact he looked forward to the nearly instantaneous effects of the anesthesia, which had extinguished his tortured mind. It was a deep, dreamless escape.

As he laid there in bed, staring at the gray sky outside the window, he began to reflect on the strange path which led him to this point, this desperate treatment in a locked psychiatric unit. How did he get here? When did it start, and how had he fallen so far, so fast? He thought about the little English boy, brutally murdered last year by two older boys, and realized that the first crack in his psyche began with that. He tried to reconstruct it, and its impact on him. He was sure now: that was the start of his flame-out, his mental and emotional disintegration. But why?

Chapter One

Matthew was employed in the production department of a large and distinguished publishing house in Boston, and he was a rising star. The top executives all knew him, and he was being carefully groomed for bigger things down the road. They'd sent him to Harvard at night for four years to pick up a post-graduate education in business administration and management. As a manager, he was a complete success, and the people who reported to him, young or old, male or female, liked and respected him because he worked so hard, listened carefully to anything they had to say, and went to bat for them. He also tried hard to help those subordinates who were struggling, either at work or in their personal lives, and on those rare occasions when he had to fire someone they knew that he'd done everything he could to try to help them to make things work, and in the end they knew and accepted their fate. One day he had three different female employees come into his office and burst into tears about matters that had nothing to do with work, or were only tangentially related. In short, Matthew was able to walk that fine line between being a friend and defending his employees, and also being a respected and responsible manager who led by example as much as anything, and who put performance and corporate responsibilities first. It was this skill of being a people-oriented, yet tough and smart executive, that led to his rapid rise through the ranks and the expectations that he would one day be a senior executive in the company, and at a relatively young age.

His home life appeared to be on the fast track, too. He had a pretty wife and two wonderful sons, aged five and three; a big Victorian home complete with Oriental rugs, antique mahogany furniture, and a swimming pool, in one of the most desirable Boston suburbs. His wife, Helen, was also rising through the ranks of the big ad agency she worked for. They had a live-in nanny who cared for the boys during the day, and on summer evenings they dined by the pool, drinking wine, and as darkness fell they lit Tiki torches and drank more wine and reveled in the ambiance. On these occasions he would sometimes think of the old cliché, "I wonder what the poor people are doing right now." He never said this aloud, because his wife had grown up in a life like this, it was her birthright and expectation, whereas he had come from a lower-class background, so different from his present life.

The only fly in the ointment, and it was a very big fly, was his marriage. There had been a distinct cooling in their relationship over the past few years. They had grown distant, and often got into arguments about ridiculous things, especially if they had a couple of glasses of wine in them. Though they still shared the same bed, they had not had sex in almost two years. They rarely did anything together any more, unless it included the boys. To Matthew, it seemed like the boys were the only area where he and Helen intersected anymore. Otherwise, they were living out separate lives, and just happened to have the same address. He would sometimes wonder if a divorce was in their future, but he always shook off the thought immediately. It was just unthinkable to him.

For some weeks now, Matthew had a growing sense that something wasn't right with him emotionally. He was anxious all the time, and sometimes he was driven to the point of tears for reasons he could not fathom. It was a general sense that something was rotting inside him, and that he was powerless to stop it.

One morning before work he sat at the kitchen table, dressed in suit and tie, drinking coffee and reading the paper, as was his habit. A story caught his eye. It was about a murder trial in England, two boys being tried for killing a four year old boy. They had lured him away from his mother at a shopping mall, then walked the crying boy, sometimes nearly dragging him, across town to a deserted area by some railroad tracks. The article described how the two boys began throwing stones and bricks at the screaming little boy, and beating him with a pipe. They kicked him until his blood spurted onto their boots. When he finally died, they left his body on the train tracks and waited and watched as a train came along and cut his body in half. They laughed at how cool it was to see his guts.

Matthew started trembling as he read the story and saw the photo of the cute little boy who'd been so brutally murdered. When he finished reading it he laid his head on the table and started sobbing uncontrollably. He felt sick to his stomach, and for a moment feared that he might vomit.

He realized that the paper was filled every day with terrible stories of murder, child abuse, stabbings, shootings, wars, genocide, natural disasters—in short, tragedy and suffering on virtually every page. He read the paper every day, and while these stories saddened him, they were merely a sort of background static in his life, just like the static of corruption in government, or the asinine antics of Hollywood celebrities, or border squabbles in the Middle East and Africa.

But this particular late summer morning, reading about the boy in England, something in Matthew gave way. He felt a large crack in his emotional foundation, and he had no idea why. The story was tragic enough, but he couldn't understand his own devastating reaction, the visceral, shattering effect it was having on him.

He pulled himself together and went to work, but something serious had definitely happened to him that morning, and the crack it had caused was so large that he became fearful that it would be seen by everyone he encountered.

That morning, he was to run a large editorial meeting for a book that was in production. He sat at the meeting, hands clasped behind his chair, and said very little. A couple of questions were directed his way, and they seemed to come at him from a hundred miles away, and he had to struggle to focus on what was being said and what was happening, what was being asked of him. He felt that his responses were acceptable, but he was not really present.

As soon as the meeting ended he took the elevator down past the eleventh floor, where his office was, all the way down to the lobby, and exited the building. "Fled" is a better word. He went to a coffee shop hidden in the bowels of a nearby office building, ordered a coffee, and once again laid his head on the table. He didn't cry, but his thoughts were only of the murder in England. He kept thinking, "Why is this murder affecting me in this way, why is it wrecking my ability to function?" He resolved that day to call Jonathan, his minister, and arrange a meeting. Perhaps Jonathan could help. He called later on and the minister agreed to meet him at the parsonage the following morning.

So, after a sleepless night, he went to the parsonage, which was really just a suburban home, a center-entrance colonial in a neighborhood of center-entrance colonials. The minister invited him in and led him to the parlor, just to the left. It was tastefully appointed, and there was nothing in it, that Matthew could see, which would identify the place as a parsonage. It was just a handsome suburban parlor. The minister sat in an easy chair on one side of the empty fireplace, and motioned for Matthew to sit in the opposite chair.

"So what brings you here?" the minister asked.

"A murder, Jonathan."

The minister looked puzzled. "A murder?"

"Yes. But don't worry, I didn't kill anyone." He paused for a moment. "Have you heard about that murder in England, the little boy who was murdered by two older boys?"

He shook his head. "No, I haven't."

Matthew told his minister about the murder, and tried to explain what had happened to him—and was still happening to him—since he'd read it. He burst into tears. When he finally calmed down, he listened while the minister talked in a bland tone about God's mysterious plan, and the unforeseen blessings which result from seemingly bad or tragic events. He also talked about free will, the gift that God had given us to choose between good and evil, and that unfortunately we sometimes do evil things. To Matthew, the minister seemed to be droning on as if reading from an all too familiar script, with blanks to be filled in with the parishioner's name and problem. The minister barely even looked at Matthew.

An urge to vomit arose in Matthew's gut. "How," he asked, "could God abandon that innocent child to hours of terror, and a horrifying death? What kind of God would use that child's agony to further his own agenda? What about the boy! Where was the merciful, loving God for him?"

The answer Matthew received, which sealed his fate, in a way, was a re-reading of the script that the minister had just read: that God works in mysterious ways; that we are not capable of understanding his plans, but that his plans are good, can only be good, despite the pain we may suffer in our ignorance.

Matthew thought again of the little boy, and wanted to spit in the minister's face, this minister whom he had always liked and respected, and who now seemed like a cardboard cut-out.

Matthew decided that day that he no longer believed in God. Or, if he did, deep down, then God was anyway a complete asshole and he wanted nothing to do with him. It was that simple. And it brought with it a feeling of sad liberation, a feeling that a world without God, or a God unworthy of worship, suddenly made so much more sense. Because a Godless world would be one where such hideous things could happen; a Godless world would be one where evil instincts could run unchecked. A Godless world would be ruled by men, or a god who was so cruel or powerless as to be an obscene joke at man's expense. And a world ruled by men or an uncaring God would result in just the sort of tragic, pathetic world we have. It was so clear now.

Unfortunately, this clarity did not lead to a resolution of his angst. In fact, most days there was an ever-strengthening psychic storm wreaking havoc in his head. Anguish, sadness, fear, anxiety and guilt swirled inside him, tearing at his seams. Even so, his brain seemed to be clogged with molasses: his ability to form coherent thoughts disintegrated, and his speech at times was slowed and almost slurred. The effects were not limited to his brain; his entire body was affected. His chest felt tight; there was a constant feeling that there was a cannon ball in his stomach; and sometimes he trembled so much that he was unable to bring a spoon of soup to his mouth without spilling it all over himself. Even his handwriting often changed and was reduced to the shaky scrawl of a ninety year old man. On top of it all, he couldn't sleep, or when he did, he woke at three or four in the morning and couldn't go back to sleep. He felt that he was literally falling apart.

At last he went to see his physician, and described what had been happening. The doctor asked him a number of questions, then told him that he was likely suffering from clinical depression.

"What is clinical depression?" Matthew asked.

"It's a neurological shift—a corruption, even—of certain areas of the brain, which leads to the sort of symptoms you've described."

"But what is the difference between depression and clinical depression?"

"Well, depression can be a normal reaction to events in a person's life. For example, you could lose a loved one, or lose your job, and you might be thrown into a depression. In most cases, this is just a normal reaction to a painful event, and passes away with time. Clinical depression, however, is a kind of blow-out in the circuitry of the brain, a physiological corruption in the pre-frontal lobe that can literally clog its ability to function. And the longer this goes on, the more the brain becomes re-wired, or corroded, and the less functional the person becomes. In time, the effects of this corrosion can become unbearable and drive a person to the edge of insanity, where suicidal urges and even psychosis become a function of life."

Matthew did not respond at first, but he identified with the doctor's explanation. Finally he asked if there was anything that could be done.

The doctor explained that there were a number of medications on the market that worked toward re-establishing the chemical balance in the brain. He prescribed a popular anti-depressant and told him to be patient because it would probably be some weeks before there was any relief.

Matthew began taking the medication but was discouraged when nothing had changed after many weeks. His misery was becoming unbearable, and he began harboring thoughts of taking his own life. It began as a small, dark secret that he carried with him everywhere. In a perverse way, the idea of killing himself became a kind of balm; being trapped in a painful existence is easier to bear when you know that you are not really trapped; that there is a an escape hatch, a way out, even if it means self destruction. Matthew carried this secret, and drew comfort from it. So much so that he began to flirt with suicide, pondering ways to do it, even to the extent of carrying out dress rehearsals.

One afternoon he walked out of his neighborhood to a nearby highway overpass. He stood watching the cars speeding under the bridge, and thought about jumping, or more accurately, how he would do it and what it would feel like. He saw the back of a large highway sign attached to the bridge, facing the cars below. It was mounted at an angle with one edge close to the bridge, and the other projecting out about six feet, connected by steel girders. He went over, sat on the railing, swung his legs over and planted his feet on the girder. With one hand still holding the railing, and his other hand extending toward the sign, he let go of the railing and carefully walked along the girder till his hand could grip the edge of the sign. He couldn't believe he was doing this. He peered around the edge of the sign and watched the on-rushing cars. He saw the startled faces of the drivers who looked up at him as they passed sixty feet below and vanished under the bridge. He imagined stepping out, letting go, and his heart beat faster as he felt the possibility draw close, reduced to a moment, the movement of a few muscles. It was exhilarating and frightening, but he was in control. He also knew it would not be long before someone in a car called 911, so he carefully returned to the railing, climbed over, and quickly made his way off the bridge. He was safe, but he was trembling all over. He was alive with death.

Another day he took an extension cord down to the basement, tied it around his neck, and tied the other end to a pipe in the ceiling. Then he stepped up onto a chair and stood there for fifteen minutes thinking about kicking away the chair, and wondering what it would be like to hang. His father had killed himself this way, and it was Matthew who had discovered him hanging from a pipe in the basement. Mathew wondered that if he did it, would he twist and kick; would his tongue protrude from his mouth; would his bowels let go? How long would he suffer? He decided that if he did kill himself, it would probably not be by hanging, as it might be too painful and slow. During that same trip to the basement he saw his electric drill, and considered the idea of drilling a hole in his head to let the sickness and the life out. But this too he rejected as being too painful and perhaps would only leave him mentally impaired instead of dead.

In the midst of all this fantasizing about suicide, he had an experience that frightened him. He was sitting on the back steps at night with a glass of wine, when a movement caught his eye. It was near a broad-leafed plant in the small garden near the pool. He got up and walked over to get a better look. When he was within a few feet of the plant, a chill passed through him, and he stopped. He stared at the plant, unable to believe his own eyes, for the leaves of the plant were slowly waving back and forth. There was no wind, and none of the other plants were moving. He stepped closer and bent down, his eyes riveted to the plant. There was no doubt about it; the broad leaves were slowly moving, curling and uncurling, moving in different directions. He felt a sickening flash of panic, but didn't move from the spot. He knew the plant wasn't really moving, and realized that he might be losing his mind. It scared the hell out of him. He turned and walked away, not looking back, and went into the house. He went straight up to his study and sat in his easy chair. He gulped his wine and sat there staring into space. He had seen a plant moving. Killing himself once again came to the fore.

A few days later he woke very early, came downstairs and turned on the coffee maker. He sat at the kitchen table, staring blankly, waiting for the coffee.

Suddenly he heard some voices. Three male voices. He couldn't make out what they were saying, but he realized with a shock that they were coming from the coffee maker. His heart rate jumped, but he didn't move. In fact, he froze, listening to the voices. He had the frightening fear, once again, that he was going insane. After a while the voices faded away. He got up and poured the coffee down the drain. Again the desire for death washed over him. He couldn't continue to live this way.

He thought of a plan which might save his family from the pain and trauma of his suicide. It would look like an accident. He'd originally considered crashing his car, but was afraid he'd survive with all sorts of permanent injuries, so he dropped the idea. He had heard, however, that drowning was certain and relatively painless—almost peaceful. He could haul his fourteen foot sloop to Winthrop, then sail from there into Boston harbor, and eventually out into the open sea. He would just sail east, the city receding behind him and disappearing below the horizon. He would sail until the inevitable storm or squall swept over and capsized his boat. He would ensure his death by not bringing a life preserver, radio, or flares, and by opening the fore and aft flotation ports so that the hull would flood and sink. Or, if he had the courage, he'd simply jump overboard and swim as far as he could until he drowned. He'd bring some booze to ease his journey across the Styx. He liked this plan because his death could be attributed to a tragic "boating accident," rather than a suicide.

He carried the idea with him for several days, but ultimately decided against it: he wanted something fast and decisive. One gray morning before work, he walked up on the Longfellow Bridge connecting Cambridge and Boston. He walked up on the bridge while subway trains and cars passed behind him, and stood at the century-old rusted railings with their peeling paint, and imagined jumping into the dark water below. Unlike the jump from the highway overpass, this jump might not bring instant death, and this bothered him. The bridge was not so high that the impact with the water would necessarily kill him; he might survive a painful impact, and then suffer the drowning. He preferred the highway bridge and a sudden death, over the river bridge.

While up on the Longfellow Bridge he was struck by the presence of some tall weeds on the other side of the railing, clinging to the few inches of crumbling concrete between the railing and oblivion. He identified with them. He was himself a weed clinging to the edge.

As he walked up the driveway that evening, he saw that Helen's car was not there; she hadn't come home from work yet. He found Jenna and the boys playing in the back yard.

"Hey, guys," was all he said, and went into the house. Jenna was now officially off-duty. He parked his briefcase, took off his jacket and tie, and poured himself three fingers of scotch. He went through the dining room to the front hall, and looked through the mail on the narrow table next to the front door. He heard Jenna and the boys coming into the back hall, by the kitchen. He quickly escaped up the front stairway to his study to relax for a few minutes before taking the kids, and closed the door. He heard Jenna come up the back stairway from the kitchen, and continue up to her room on the third floor. Her room was directly above his study, and he heard her footsteps as she moved about the room.

Jenna was a twenty-two year old girl from Iowa. She'd been a runner up in the Miss Iowa pageant a few years before, just before she'd come east to be their nanny. She'd had a great resume, excellent recommendations from the agency, and the several telephone interviews with her had gone well. Helen and he had both felt good about hiring her. But from the moment Matthew had looked at the photos Jenna had sent of herself, he realized there was an added element to his desire to hire her that Helen had not considered. Namely, that Jenna was drop-dead gorgeous. Not only that, but as he looked into her eyes in the close-up photos, he saw The Look. He knew instantly that she was no naïve virgin. He saw sex in her eyes. Of course, he was a married man, and she would be an employee, but the thought of this vixen living in his home, a part of his daily life, and that he'd get to see her every day, was a sweet bonus. So he enthusiastically endorsed Helen's desire to hire her.

As it turned out, Jenna was indeed a fine nanny. She grew to truly love the boys, and they her. Jenna also fell in love with Boston. Being a small-town Iowan, Boston was almost a dreamy foreign country for her, and when she was off duty she almost always headed out the door to meet up with friends she'd made—most of them nannies or au pairs she'd met through the agency or the neighborhood playgrounds—and hit the club scene in Boston or Cambridge. Many evenings, as he watched her cheerily come down the stairs in a mini-skirt, stockings and high heels, he wished more than anything to be young and free, free to go out with her. Instead, as he hunched over a cup of coffee or an after-dinner glass of wine, he could only watch as she disappeared out the door into the night, into a life he had never had and would never know. But this particular evening, something happened which lit a fire in Matthew. Or at least he thought something had happened; but he realized it was possible he'd read something devilish into a completely innocent event, because he was wearing devil-colored glasses when it came to Jenna. What happened is this: after downing his scotch—rather quickly—he'd gone downstairs and found Michael, his three year old, in the parlor. He decided to get down on the floor and engage in some physical play. He knew Michael would love it, and he could lose himself in his love for Michael.

A few minutes later Jenna came downstairs. He could tell by the sound of her steps that she was in high heels. Then she came into the parlor. Matthew at that moment was lying on his back in front of the fireplace, holding Michael in the air. They were playing airplane, one of Michael's favorite games, and Michael had his arms outstretched and his legs straight out and was grinning ear to ear as Matthew turned him back and forth, up and down. Matthew glanced at Jenna, and his heart jumped. She was wearing a short skirt with nude stockings and high heels. What happened next set his loins on fire. There was a large mirror over the mantle, and she moved in front of it to check herself out and fluff her beautiful blonde hair. She was standing no more than three feet from Matthew's head, her perfectly shaped legs rising up, converging in the dark oval of her short hemline. He thought she must know he could see up her dress. Then he raised his eyes to the mirror and saw that she was looking right back into his eyes, and her look seemed to say, "You want to fuck me, don't you."

Oh my god, he thought, and felt a surge of electricity. He had to look away.

They didn't exchange a word. Jenna finished doing whatever she was doing, then turned and stepped over Matthew's legs. Again the dark vortex of her thighs. She squatted down, her knees to one side, her skirt riding up her thighs, and looking at Michael she smiled and poked him in the belly, which drew a giggle. "Thank you for being such a good boy today. I'll see you later, alligator."

Michael grinned. "In a while, crocodile."

Jenna looked Matthew in the eyes, a bit too long, he thought, and then she smiled. She stood up and left the room. Matthew just laid there listening to the sound of her heels as she passed through the kitchen, the back hall, and out the door. His thoughts were racing. He wondered if something had just happened here, or if his libido had over-reacted, reading something into nothing. He smiled at Michael and resumed their airplane game, but his mind was on Jenna. He noticed that his arms were trembling.

When he saw Jenna again the next day, Saturday, he was excited and nervous and guilt-ridden. Something positive had entered his mind, and it was like water to a man dying of thirst. His nerves were poised to pick up the slightest signal from her, but there was nothing. Her words, her looks, her body language were completely devoid of anything but her normal friendliness to her employer. Matthew felt disappointed, but somehow relieved too. Nothing in subsequent days stirred things, and he became more and more convinced that he'd misread things that day in the parlor, that he'd had a bit to drink and had simply let his lust cloud his judgment.

The following weekend Matthew had the house all to himself as Helen and the boys had gone to an out-of-state family reunion for the weekend. Matthew had declined to go, partly because he was depressed and didn't feel able to handle all the parties and socializing, and partly because he relished the idea of a quiet, peaceful weekend at home, alone with his books. He knew too that Jenna was rarely around on weekends, except when she came home late at night to crash.

It had been cloudy and cool that Saturday, and it being September, he decided to have the first fire of the season and spend the evening reading before its crackling warmth. He loved to read in the parlor with a fire going. The only time he left the house that day was to buy a bottle of cognac.

He brought down several books from the study, poured himself a healthy cognac and spent the evening just as he'd hoped. Before long he felt himself becoming suffused with a mellow warmth from both the cognac and the fire. From time to time he would look up from his book and stare at the fire. It was mesmerizing. He felt relaxed and content, a rare experience for him these days.

Around ten he was surprised to hear Jenna come in the back door; she usually stayed out till the wee hours. He heard her heels coming through the kitchen, and then she came into the parlor.

"Oh, hi Matthew."

"Hi, Jenna."

She looked at the fire and smiled. "Oh, that's so nice. I love fires."

She was dressed in a short burgundy dress, and her shapely legs were bare. Matthew could tell by her eyes and her voice that she'd had a few drinks, as had he.

"Did you have a nice time?" he asked.

"It was okay. We just kind of fizzled early tonight." She looked at the fire again. "We always had fires at home. Sometimes I'd just lie on the rug and stare at it for hours."

"Be my guest."

She smiled. "Really? I won't disturb you?"

"Not at all." He grabbed the blanket by his side on the sofa and held it out. "Here. Just spread this on the floor. Make yourself comfortable."

"Thank you, Matthew. I promise I won't stay long."

"Stay as long as you want. Really. I'm just reading and enjoying my cognac."

She glanced at his glass on the end table. "I'm embarrassed to ask this," she said, "but what exactly is cognac? I mean, I've heard of it, but I've never had it."

Matthew lifted his snifter. "Well, it's hard to describe. It's made of grapes, like wine, but it's very intense and has a lot more alcohol. Sort of like a cross between wine and a good scotch, but about half the alcohol of scotch. It's made in the Cognac region of France. It's made in the U.S. too, but they can't call it cognac. The American version is called brandy, and it's not nearly as good. This particular cognac," he said, raising the snifter, "was the favorite of Napoleon." He felt quite suave as he explained all this.

"I like the glass," she said, looking at it.

"This is a glass just for cognac, a snifter. In fact, if you really want to be proper about it, you can put the snifter in a special holder with a candle under it, and it warms the cognac. There's nothing quite like a warm cognac, especially on a cold winter night."

"Really," she said. "That's so cool." Then she giggled. "Wait, that didn't come out right."

Matthew laughed. He held out the snifter. "Go ahead, give it a try. Give it a sniff first. The glass holds the scent."

She sniffed the cognac, then tilted it back and took a healthy sip. "Mmm. Wow. I like it. It's strong, but I like it."

He wasn't sure if she really liked it, or was just being polite, but he decided to ask her if she wanted more. "How about I pour you a cognac while you get yourself comfortable in front of the fire?" He was already on his feet.

"I'd like that, Matthew. Thank you."

"Let me get you a snifter. I'll be right back." He felt like skipping out of the room. He and Jenna sharing cognac before the fire, just the two of them. Maybe they won't even talk, but god, just to look at her! He knew tonight in bed that he'd be fantasizing about making love to her. He actually felt happy. He poured her a copious amount of cognac, and trying not to look giddy, returned to the parlor. She was sitting on the sofa, undoing the ankle straps of her high heels, and the sight sent a thrill through his body. He handed her the snifter.

"Mmm, thank you." She had spread the blanket before the fireplace, and taking a small pillow from the sofa, she stood and walked in her bare feet onto the blanket. With a feminine elegance, she knelt down, placed her snifter on the floor, and laid down on her right side, with her hand propping her head. Her golden locks glowed in the firelight and tumbled down over her arm and shoulders. Her entire body, from her feet to her hair, was silhouetted by the fire. Her curves were so perfect that Matthew fell into a state of aroused awe. He gulped a mouthful of cognac, and sank into a reverie that excluded everything but the poetry of her body and the excitement coursing through his veins. There was no way he could read with Jenna lying there before him. His whole body was tingling with desire. He knew that nothing could happen between them, yet he reveled in the fantasy. He watched as periodically she raised the snifter and sipped.

After a while she took another sip and suddenly looked back over her shoulder at him. His gaze froze: she'd caught him staring. He should have been reading, he should have at least lowered his eyes, but he couldn't. His eyes held her gaze for what seemed an eternity. He felt his face flush.

Finally, there were words. Her voice was low, almost a whisper. "This is nice, Matthew."

Matthew's throat constricted. The words came out on their own. "You don't have to stay there on the floor. The sofa is very comfortable." He moved his hand over the sofa next to him.

She said nothing, but picked up her snifter and came over to the sofa.

Matthew was speechless, but he patted the sofa next to him, still gazing into her eyes.

She sat down next to him, their thighs almost touching. A sense of panic rose in him. He wondered what the hell he was doing, and where it would lead. He was on some sort of dangerous peak, and he didn't know which way he was going to fall. He looked at Jenna, raised his snifter, and said, "Here's to fires."

Jenna smiled, and touched her glass to his. "To fires."

Their eyes locked and they remained that way as they sipped their cognac. Finally Matthew lowered his eyes; the heat was too intense. He looked at the fire, wondering what to do. Should he try to seduce her? Should he just enjoy the flirtation, try to draw it out because it felt so wonderful being with this gorgeous young woman who was engaging in a heated dance with him, and then stop it before the point of no return? Yes, that's what he'd do. He'd dance, and then he'd walk away. It was the right thing to do. He thought of Helen, and told himself that he was a married man, that this girl was their nanny, and it would surely end in disaster if he tried to seduce her. Yes; he would simply enjoy his drink with her and then retire for the night.

"This is so nice," she said. She was looking at the fire as well. They were silent for a long, pregnant moment. Then she said, "You know, you have it all, Matthew. A beautiful home, two wonderful children, a nice wife. I hope I can have a life like this someday."

Matthew took a sip from his glass. "Looks can be deceiving," he said.

She looked at him. "What do you mean?"

"Well, I'm sure you've noticed that Helen and I have our problems. With our marriage. Would you believe we haven't made love for two years?" Matthew regretted saying it; he felt he was playing for sympathy, and he didn't feel right about sharing his marital problems with Jenna. But with his mouth fueled by alcohol, he couldn't stop. "I think I'm a sensuous person; sex is important to me. Yet sex for me now is, well, my right hand." He couldn't believe he'd actually said that.

"You deserve better," she said. There was a long pause. "If I had a man like you, I'd want to show him every night how appreciative I am."

Matthew's heart rate increased even more. He looked at her, and once again their eyes locked, unblinking.

"I fantasize about you," he said. He couldn't believe the things he was saying. He knew that he was now entering dangerous territory, yet he felt powerless to stop.

"I've fantasized about you, too," she said. "Many times."

For a long moment they sat there looking into each other's eyes. He wanted to kiss her. This is it, he thought. This is the line, and I am about to cross it. "May I kiss you?"

"Yes," she said, almost in a whisper.

With fire coursing through his every vein, he leaned toward her, and she toward him, and they kissed. It was a long, beautiful kiss. Matthew was in bliss.

A few minutes later he was kneeling on the floor before her, his body between her legs. She was still sitting, but she'd slid down so that the bottom of her dress was even with her crotch, revealing the black satin panties she was wearing. She put her hands around his head and drew him toward the black triangle between her legs. He opened his mouth and pressed his tongue, then his mouth, into the already moist fabric, the black film that separated his tongue from the paradise on the other side. She sighed deeply, with the hint of a moan. He looked up and saw that her head was thrown back, her mouth open, her eyes closed. He was becoming mad with desire. He slid his hands up the outside of her thighs, up to her hips, across the narrow waistband of her panties, and hooked his fingers on them. Slowly, he pulled them down her thighs; she lifted her legs and he pulled the tiny panties off first one leg, then the other, and dropped them on the floor. Her sex was revealed, open before him, inches from his face. He leaned in and pushed his tongue into her. They were both panting. Jenna began to writhe, grinding her sex against his mouth, his teeth, his darting tongue. He leaned back slightly, and inserted his finger into her. She groaned. Matthew was so aroused that he felt he might ejaculate in his pants. He pulled away, sitting back on his heels, panting. He looked at the vortex of her silky thighs, the mound of soft hair, her dress pushed up to her waist, her lovely face in ecstasy. He wanted so badly to make love to her, to feel himself thrusting inside of her. But suddenly a monstrous wave of guilt rolled over him, sweeping him away. A voice in his head said "Stop! Don't do it! Stop while you still can!" He actually shook his head, as if trying to clear it. Suddenly, he stood up and dropped onto the sofa next to her. "Jenna, I can't do this. I want to make love to you so bad, but I just can't do this." His head fell back against the sofa. He turned his head and looked at her. Her eyes were pools of desire. She placed her hand on his crotch, and rubbed the stiffness through his pants, and almost against his will he thrust his hips up to meet her hand. "Let me do this for you," she said.

He was about to nod yes, then, once again, the voice in his head told him to stop, right now, before it was too late. "Jenna," he said. "I want you so much.

Believe me, I do. You are so incredibly beautiful and sexy. You're like a dream come true. But we can't do this. It will only lead to big trouble for both of us."

Jenna pulled her hand away, sighed, then lifted her hips and pulled her dress down. She looked at him. "I know. I know. I just can't help myself. You're just so hot."

Matthew chuckled. "I'm nothing compared to you. Oh my god, you are so beautiful and sexy. I must be out of my mind to turn down this chance with you." They were holding hands now.

"Lust is a powerful thing, isn't it?" she said, smiling.

"Yes. Lust and alcohol are a dangerous combination."

"Add a cozy fire to the mix, and you're practically doomed."

They both laughed.

"Seriously, though," Matthew continued. "If I made love to you now, I know I couldn't possibly do it just once. I'd be looking for every opportunity to be alone with you, and sooner or later we'd get caught."

"I know. I know," she said. "My mind is telling me one thing, but my body is telling me another."

He chuckled. "Yeah. Tell me about it."

He was so absorbed in their conversation that for a moment the sound of the back door opening didn't register. Then it hit him like a blast of icy air. "Oh my god," he said, abruptly sitting up. "Helen's home! Fuck!" They both jumped to their feet. He whirled around in panic, not knowing what to do. He saw Jenna trying to kick her panties under the sofa. "Sit down!" he whispered hoarsely. They both sat, this time with some distance between them. A second later, Helen came into the room. She stopped, and a look of surprise came over her as she saw the two of them. She looked at the blanket on the floor.

"Oh, hi, Hon," Matthew said. "What are you doing here?" He felt flush, and there was a slight quiver in his voice despite his desperate effort to seem calm.

Helen looked at Matthew, then Jenna, then back at Matthew. "I might ask the same of the two of you."

"Oh, we're just having a drink. Jenna just got home a few minutes ago. She'd never had cognac—can you believe it?—so I gave her one to try."

"Well, I'm exhausted," Jenna said, and stood up. "Thanks for the cognac," she said, glancing at Matthew. He saw the fear in her eyes. "Good night," she said, as she walked out of the room. He heard her bare feet on the steps. Helen just stood there, staring at him.

"You bastard," she hissed.

His feigned shock was mixed with horror and fear. "Why? What are you talking about?"

"You're full of shit. You know goddam well what I'm talking about. How could you stoop so low? Our own nanny? Well, I guess I know how you could, because you're a fucking bastard."

"Helen, we didn't do anything," he said, in an imploring tone. "I know it might've looked like it, but I swear nothing was going on. She literally came home just a few minutes before you did."

Helen had a sneering, disgusted look on her face. "Then you two must have been going at it mighty quick."

"Why do you say that? We weren't doing anything . . . just talking."

"Oh, and while you were talking, her panties just accidentally fell off."

"What are you talking about?"

She pointed at the bottom edge of the sofa.

Matthew leaned forward and looked down. A sickening feeling hit him hard, for there, on the rug, halfway under the sofa, were Jenna's panties. She had failed to kick them all the way under. Matthew's throat constricted, and he couldn't respond. The game was up, and he didn't know what to say. He couldn't look at Helen; he just hung his head. Helen left the room and he heard her go out the back door, presumably to get the boys, who were no doubt asleep in the car. Matthew felt sick to his stomach. He felt doomed. He gulped down his cognac, and Jenna's too. He picked up Jenna's panties, stood up and stuffed them in his pocket. Then he went outside to help Helen with the boys. He picked up Michael and followed Helen, who was carrying Justin, into the house and up the kitchen stairway to their bedrooms. Neither of them said a word. Matthew was frightened. He knew it was only the eye of the storm. As he came out of Michael's room he thought of poor Jenna upstairs, knowing that Helen was going to fire her. He went back downstairs and into the parlor. He picked up the blanket, rolled it up and tossed it on the floor beside the sofa, and sat down. A few minutes later he heard Helen coming down the front stairway. She came into the parlor and stood looking at him. Matthew hung his head. "Helen, I'm so sorry. I am so sorry." She didn't respond, and he sat there looking at the fire. "I know you're not going to believe this, but we didn't have sex. We were fooling around, but we stopped. We stopped before you came home, not because you came home."

"You're not only a fucking bastard and a cheat, you're also a fucking liar."

Matthew didn't know what to say.

"Get out," Helen said.

"What?"

"Get out," she repeated. Her voice was rising, getting angrier. "Get out! Get out of here! You make me sick!" She was shouting now. "Get the fuck out of here!"

Matthew stood up. He felt anger rising in his own gut, though he wasn't sure why. He grabbed his empty snifter and whipped it across the room, where it exploded against the wall, tearing the wallpaper. "Fine! That's what you want? You got it!" He brushed past her and stalked out of the room, through the kitchen, and into the back hall. He was drunk and explosive. He kicked his foot through the plexiglass storm door, and half ran to his car. He slammed the car door, started it, and backed down the driveway at speed. He pulled into the street and with a squeal of rubber tore up the street, not knowing where he was going except away from home.

He drove aimlessly for a while, trembling. He stopped to buy a bottle of scotch, and drove to a nearby motel. He booked a room, which was borderline sleazy, then sat on the bed staring into space, breathing heavily and taking swigs from the bottle. Finally he fell back on the bed and passed out.

At some point during the early hours he woke up. He was in the same position. It was still dark outside. A torrent of emotions rushed over him: guilt; anger; confusion; a sense of being lost. He had a pounding headache. He felt that he was beginning to scrape bottom, and he didn't know what to do about it. He felt ready to explode. He gulped down some more scotch, then staggered into the bathroom. He took another swig from the bottle, then poured the rest of it into a couple of the motel glasses. Then he smashed the bottle on the edge of the sink. There was glass everywhere. He picked up a large shard and began hacking his left wrist until blood was streaming down his arm into the sink and all over the floor. Then he dipped his finger into the wounds and, as if finger painting, drew a swastika on his cheek. Then he drew a cross on his other cheek. He stared at himself in the mirror and felt a queer satisfaction, a kind of release. A kind of calm. He pulled several feet from the roll of toilet paper and wrapped it around his bleeding wrist. The tissue quickly stained with blood, and he grabbed some more paper and wrapped his whole forearm tightly ten or twenty times until the blood was stanched and a sense of clean tightness replace the pain and blood. He was calm now, the cutting having afforded him a catharsis of sorts. He spent a few minutes wiping up the blood and collecting the shards of glass from the floor. He threw away the glass and dropped the bloody towels into the sink. He was ashamed and relieved at the same time. He had done this before, and felt the same sort of relief. It was not an attempt at suicide, but an outlet for the overload of pain he felt. He'd told himself before after cutting himself that it was the last time, even as he knew that he'd do it again when the impulse was strong enough.

He went into the bedroom and climbed into bed drunk and fully clothed. He replayed the scenes with Jenna and with Helen, but soon fell into a fitful sleep populated by a succession of nightmares. At one point he woke himself up with a scream. The only thing he could remember was his looking into a mirror and seeing his face dissolving into a mass of skinless muscle and bone. He fell asleep again.

In the morning he awoke with a smashing headache and an overpowering sense of self-disgust. He thought about blowing his brains out, but there was the problem of not having a gun. He looked at his wrist, wrapped in toilet paper which had become a soggy, bloody mess. He retrieved one of the glasses of scotch from the bathroom and drank. A few minutes later he was starting to feel better. A little hair of the dog. He walked unsteadily to the motel office and booked his room for several more days. Then he returned to his room, hung a "Do Not Disturb" sign on the door handle, and resumed drinking. After a while he turned on the TV and paid to watch a porn film. A few minutes in, he became aroused, unzipped his pants, and made himself come. Afterwards, he felt dirty and ashamed. Here he was, lying in a cheap motel room with semen all over his stomach, and one arm bandaged in bloody toilet paper. The memory of his clash with Helen was a raw wound. He wondered if he could sink any lower. The only thing that came to mind was suicide. Escape, escape, escape. It became a sort of mantra. But once again he felt caught between Scylla and Charybdis; too weak to live, and too weak to die. This must be purgatory, he thought, with the sulfuric fumes of Hell in his nostrils.

He spent the morning in his room, drinking. He was in a kind of stupor, fuelled by alcohol and misery. At last, around noon, he stirred from the bed and called home. Helen answered the phone.

"Hi," was all he could muster.
"What do you want?"
"Can you forgive me?" he asked, his voice sounding broken.
"No, I can't."
"What about Jenna?"
"What about her? I fired her."
Matthew's heart sank. "She didn't do anything wrong," he said, weakly.
"She did enough."
There was a long pause. "Can I come home?"
"No, you cannot come home. We're through."
"What are you saying?"
"I want a divorce. That's what I'm saying."
The phone dropped from Matthew's hand. He felt sick. He picked up the phone. "Is that what you really want?"
"Yes. It's exactly what I want. Let's face it, Matt. Our marriage died long ago."
He was silent for a long moment. His eyes were welling up. "What about the boys?" he said at last.

"What about them?"

"I mean, what are you going to tell them?" His voice was trembling, and tears were beginning to flow.

"I'll figure it out," she said, curtly. "Don't worry, you'll still get to see them. For their sake. Not yours."

He was silent for a moment. Tears were rolling down his cheeks. He could barely speak. "I'm at the Patriot Arms in Cambridge, if you want to reach me."

"Good. My attorney will know where to find you, then."

"Your attorney?" Matthew was stunned by the swiftness of it all. "You're really going to do this, end it all, after all these years?"

"You ended it the other night. Remember that?"

"Helen, I'm so sorry." His mind was reeling.

"Matthew, you're a selfish bastard." She hung up the phone.

He started sobbing violently. He couldn't believe all this was happening. He was in shock. And poor Jenna. She was just a young kid who'd had a bit too much to drink and fell prey to his lust. Now she was out of a job. And the kids had loved her so much. He had ruined everything.

He crawled back into bed. He felt so ashamed and disgusted. He stared at the ceiling for a long time. He had the frightening, overwhelming feeling that today was the first day of the rest of his life.

Chapter Two

Matthew stayed at the motel a few more days. He'd called in sick to the office, and spent his time either drinking or looking for a small apartment to rent, or both. He found a studio in a non-descript brick building with a dozen units, and it was only a mile from his house and the boys. And he'd have the same commute to work. He made sure Helen was not home when he made trips to the house to pick up clothing and belongings. It saddened him deeply each time he entered the empty house, walking from room to room, looking at family photos, decorations, furniture. This was his home, be he felt like a stranger to it now, an intruder who didn't belong there. Sometimes he wept.

He returned to work the following week, and though nicely dressed and groomed as always, he looked so terrible that no one even doubted whether he'd really been sick. His depression continued to deepen; he was in the proverbial downward spiral. The days stretched into weeks, and the agony continued. It began to affect his work. He stayed in his office as much as possible, avoiding meetings and interactions with others. He often closed his office door, something he rarely did in the past. He'd close the door and rest his head on his folded arms. Even worse, because he was no longer able to concentrate or think clearly, he was making mistakes. Some of them serious. His bosses were shocked. Matthew was shocked too. But the more he struggled, the more felt that he was being sucked deeper into some black morass.

One morning, on the subway ride downtown, Matthew kept his sunglasses on, partly because he didn't want anyone to see the anguish in his eyes, and partly because the darkness they offered made him feel cocooned, separate from the normal world around him. He knew that to the other passengers, who could not see his eyes or read his thoughts, he too looked normal. He was dressed smartly in tan slacks, a blue Oxford shirt, a navy blazer, a burgundy, blue and tan tie, and shined cordovan loafers. He looked the part he was so desperately trying to play; that of the thirty-something executive commuting from the suburbs to a genteel job in Boston. But looks, he knew, can be deceiving. When he looked at a star at night, he knew that the light had taken so long to reach Earth, to reach him, that he was really looking into the past, seeing the star as it was thousands or millions of years ago. In fact, the star may have exploded long ago. Yet there it was, twinkling in the sky. And so it was with Matthew: his star was still shining for all to see, but in reality he was already gone.

The subway train pulled into the Park Street station. Normally he would have gotten off, transferred to a green-line trolley, and walked one block to the office. Today, he was unable to get out of his seat. He watched the mass exodus of well-dressed executives and secretaries, and suddenly felt like a truant. He was going to stay on the train. He was going to play hookie. Though it was a choice he made, it didn't feel like a choice at all. It felt like a necessity. He could not possibly have gotten off the train and made it to the office. He didn't have the strength to do it. So he stayed in his seat, and when the doors closed, he felt relieved. It was done.

But what now? He didn't know. All he knew was that he was going to keep riding. And so he did. And as the train made its way across the city, depositing more and more passengers, and taking on fewer and fewer, he realized he would soon be heading out of the city, out to the South Shore suburbs he was unfamiliar with, and at some point, he'd reach the end of the line. And what then? He didn't really care. He was only relieved that he was still on the train, and not walking with the hordes of office workers toward his building or others nearby. He was on an adventure, with no goal or destination in mind. He was not running toward anything; he was running away from everything. And it felt good.

So he stayed on the train, stop after stop, as it gradually emptied and made its way out of the city toward the South Shore. The last stop was in Braintree. By then the train was virtually empty. He had no choice but to get up and get off. As he stood on the platform he felt alone and free. "No one knows where I am," he thought. But the sense of relief was soon replaced by guilt. What was he doing? He had a job to do, people to manage, problems to solve. Yet he was still constantly tormented by the murder of the English boy, or thoughts of the night with Jenna. Above all, he was haunted by thoughts of killing himself.

Suicide presented itself everywhere he turned now. There were bridges to jump off of, pharmacies full of sleeping pills and razor blades, trees to slam into while driving. The opportunities were endless. And thinking of them thrilled him. Death was his escape hatch, his ticket to merciful oblivion. All his anguish, sadness, depression, and anxiety; all his doubts and fears and responsibilities; all his failures, moral transgressions and guilt; all of it could be wiped away. It was a beautiful thought.

Yet this thought only compounded his guilty feelings. How could he possibly kill himself when he had two young sons? How could he destroy their lives by taking his own and leaving behind a legacy of pain that would sear them forever? His boys were the most precious, most beautiful things in his life. How could he wreck their lives by taking his own? He felt trapped.

But he was also good at rationalizing things. He'd done it his whole life. It frightened him that at times he was able to rationalize his suicide in spite of the boys. He would tell himself that he was not really there for them anymore. That his suicide would not affect them the way his own father's suicide had affected him. He told himself that Helen was a strong woman, a strong mother: she would guide them through it. She would, in time, help them to understand that their father was ill, he was in pain, and not in his right mind. They might not ever accept it, but at least they would understand. And they would be financially secure because he's established a trust fund for them, and ensured that there were no suicide clauses in his life insurance policies. So the boys, and Helen, would have all the money they'd ever need. They would be millionaires several times over.

He thought about these things as he sat on the platform waiting for a return train. He decided he would go to the office after all, but something had changed. He was outside the fold now. He was frightened, yet strangely calm and focused. He was filled with a sense of purpose, for the first time in a long time. On the ride back into the city he allowed himself to luxuriate in the thoughts that today was the day, the long dreaded and long awaited day.

When he finally arrived at his stop, he left the train and rode the escalator to the street. It was ten o'clock—still fairly early. He noticed as he approached his office building that his legs were trembling, and each step became more difficult. It was like walking in lead shoes. Yet he now had the strength to keep going. He entered the building as into the mouth of a furnace, but he had a purpose now, and he could go on. He rode the elevator to his department and, avoiding any contact with others, slipped into his office and closed the door. He knew there would be a score of phone messages and e-mails awaiting him, and it felt good to ignore them, to know that he'd never have to deal with the problems they represented. He was done now. His phone rang, and he ignored it. He had something important to do.

He opened a drawer, took out a few sheets of stationery, and began writing a suicide note. He found it surprisingly easy to do.

To Justin, Michael, Helen and anyone else who cares:
Let me say first that I am deeply sorry for the pain my death will cause for those who love me. Suicide is a terrible thing for those left behind—as I well know—and from the bottom of my miserable heart I beg that you will try to forgive me. And perhaps the only way you can ever forgive me is to understand why I have decided to end my life.

The short answer is that I am sick, and my sickness makes living a kind of private hell which has eroded my will to withstand it anymore.

I realize that my life, on the surface, is a good one: I have two wonderful sons, a wife who was always good to me and is a great mother to our children, a good job, good bodily health, and no material wants. There are so many people who would give their all to have what I have, and would say that I have been very "blessed" or fortunate, or both. Unfortunately my illness robs me of the joy a healthy person would derive from these things. It shuts me off, alienates me from everyone and everything, including my own self. It shuts me in, trapping me inside the walls of my sickness. When others admire the beauty of a warm, spring day, I only feel worse because I cannot experience it; it only reminds me of my own dark, polluted state.

For me, all too often, the sheer act of being conscious, of being alive, is to endure an overwhelmingly tangled mess of depression, anxiety, guilt, sadness, anger, insecurity, exhaustion, fear, confusion and anguish, from the moment I open my eyes in the morning till the moment I go to sleep at night (and often beyond, in my horrific nightmares).

I am not trying to drum up pity here; I am only trying to give some idea of the mental and emotional life I have tried my very best to endure. And the fact is, I can no longer fight the battle. To fight takes strength, and I have none left. I am tired now, tired and worn out.

Helen, you once took the Beck Depression Index test at my request, and your score was a three. A three. Even in my healthiest, happiest moments I would never come close to a score that low. Clinical depression starts at seventeen; my scores are typically in the high thirties (severe depression) or forties (extreme depression). That's what I live with every day, while still struggling to be a normal human being.

When the simple act of putting gas into my car or having a thirty-second conversation with another human being becomes an overwhelming task that requires great effort on my part, the toll on my psyche quickly becomes intolerable and exhausting. Undoubtedly this is a result of my illness. Furthermore, healthy people do not hear voices emanating from their coffee-makers and see plants moving around.

Frankly, I've had enough of all this—I've no strength left to fight it anymore. Life—such a precious gift that so many people covet—has for me become an on-going torture. I am desperate for relief, for peace. And the only relief I see is death.

I do not believe in an afterlife. I believe we are merely animals with a more highly developed brain, and that we are born, we live, and we die, just like any other animal, insect or plant. And that is a great comfort to me as I face my own death. Oblivion is what I seek, not some pseudo-retirement community in the sky.

Let me end this by saying again that I am deeply, deeply sorry for causing anyone pain; I hope you will try to remember good things about me, that I tried to be a good person, a loving father and husband, and to be compassionate. I have tried to explain in this letter how it is that I've been driven to do such a terrible thing as commit suicide. I don't know if you'll ever understand, just as I struggled to understand my father's suicide for many years. But now I understand, if he experienced the same anguish that I've struggled with. Understanding is the key to forgiveness. But I am saddened to think that you might never truly understand, and therefore never forgive me for this terrible act. I know that you will be angry and hurt. I know, Justin and Michael, that you are too young to understand any of this. But perhaps when you are older, this letter will help.

But please, please know that I love you all deeply, and that, at bottom, it is my illness that has eaten and eroded my insides and taken me to this moment of saying goodbye. I simply cannot live like this any longer.

With all my love, from the bottom of my heart,
Matthew/Dad

After completing the note, he made another copy. He put one in the pocket of his blazer; the other he placed in his briefcase. He did this because he planned to die under the wheels of a subway train, and in case his body (and the note) were completely mutilated, there would be a copy of it in his briefcase, which he would leave in his office.

With the notes tucked away, he surveyed his desk, then swept everything off it into the trash can. "*C'est fini*," he said. He opened his door slightly, made sure the hall was clear, then quickly made his way to the elevator. He rode down alone, as he had hoped, and exited the building into the bright, clear morning. He felt a tremendous sense of relief, even giddiness. He was free. He was severing all the bonds connecting him to the world. He was shedding everything for this freedom, this free act of ending his life.

When he reached the entrance of the Park Street station, he turned and took a last look at the people, the trees, the buildings, the sky. They still seemed distant and colorless, but it didn't bother him. He felt calm, almost detached, from everything, including himself. He went down into the station, bought his token, and passed through the turn-style. He headed left to where the tracks from the tunnels are level with the station platform. This meant he would not have to jump down. All he had to do was walk around an iron fence warning people off, then walk right onto the tracks and into the dark tunnel. And so he did. He wondered how many people might have seen him enter the tunnel. Perhaps no one had noticed; it was, after all, a big, busy station. As he continued into the darkness he felt safe now; no one had tried to stop him. The tunnel was only dimly lit, and as he walked along the track, along the blackened gravel and ties between the rails, he was conscious of the incongruity between how he looked, and where he was. A sharp-dressed man, his tie neatly knotted, walking into the deepening darkness of a subway tunnel, soon to be killed by a train.

Then he heard it. The train. He could hear and feel it coming. He had walked around a bend in the tunnel, so there was no real light yet, but he knew it was coming. The noise and vibration grew stronger, and suddenly the tunnel was filled with light and he could see his own shadow in the track bed before him growing longer by the instant. He didn't look back. He kept on walking. His heart was racing now. He heard a horn and the screeching of brakes, and expected at any second to feel a violent slam from behind, perhaps an instant of pain and then—nothing. Sweet nothing. Sweet death. He'd be a mess for someone else to clean up.

The tunnel was brilliant now, and the screeching pierced him. And then... nothing. Silence and light. But he wasn't dead. The train had stopped in time. Matthew stopped as well. He'd failed. His life had been spared. He stood there for some moments, then turned around and through the glare of its headlight, saw that the train was no more than a few feet away. The driver was staring at him, his mouth open, a look of consternation and shock on his face. Matthew calmly walked the narrow space between the train and the tunnel wall, past the passengers gawking at him through the illuminated windows, and back out into the station. He felt disappointed, but detached from it all and strangely calm. He was devoid of emotion. He walked downstairs to the lower platform and boarded a Red Line train just before the doors closed. In a kind of numb stupor he rode as far as Harvard Square. In the Square he felt his whole body beginning to tremble. He suddenly felt as if a bucket of ice water had been dumped on him. He'd done something very stupid and dangerous, and the healthy side of him, however small, knew that he needed help. He stopped at a payphone and dialed 911. He calmly explained to the operator that he'd walked into a subway tunnel, hoping to die, and answered her questions about his location. While he was still on the phone, a police car pulled up in front of him. An officer gently grasped his elbow. "Mr. St. Clare?"

"Yes," he said. He told the 911 operator that the police had come, and thanked her. As he hung up, an ambulance pulled up behind the patrol car, its lights flashing. He was amazed at the speed of the response. The back doors opened, and the policeman, still holding his elbow, escorted him to the ambulance, and with the assistance of an EMT, he climbed into the back. The policeman looked at him and said, "You did the right thing, calling us. You're going to be okay."

Matthew's heart stirred with gratitude. Perhaps the officer was right.

Chapter Three

Matthew was taken to Mt. Auburn Hospital, in Cambridge, and given a bed in a private room. A police officer was stationed outside his door, and when Matthew attempted to leave the room to find a doctor, the officer placed his hand on Matthew's chest, and said, "You can't leave this room." Matthew nodded, and returned to his bed.

At last a doctor came in and asked him a litany of questions. When he'd finished, he told Matthew that he was going to be transferred to McLean Hospital. Matthew immediately thought of Sylvia Plath, Anne Sexton and Robert Lowell, all of whom had spent time there. It was no consolation; no lessoning of his fear. It was just a fact.

An hour later he was escorted to a waiting ambulance. The EMT strapped his arms and legs to the bed. Matthew stared at the ceiling of the ambulance for the duration of the ride to McLean, which was only about fifteen minutes.

He went through an admissions process that lasted hours, and included meetings with a couple of psychiatrists. They both asked the same questions: why did you do it; how long had you been having suicidal thoughts; how long have you been depressed; can you think of anything that might have triggered it; was there something that triggered you today to try to kill yourself, and on and on. Matthew tried to answer their questions as honestly and openly as he could. He even described the incidents where he'd seen the moving plant, and had heard voices in the coffee-maker. Both of them told him what he already knew, that he was clinically depressed, with psychotic episodes. A nurse attached a band around his wrist with a label that had his name, patient ID number, and some other numbers he didn't understand. She also gave him a glossy McLean folder that contained some information about the hospital.

Finally, in the early evening, he was escorted upstairs to a locked psychiatric unit. A nurse greeted him and led him down the hall to the nurses' station. She asked him to sit while she took his temperature and checked his blood pressure.

She made notations on a clipboard. Then she asked him to step onto a scale, and noted his weight.

"Okay, Matthew, let me give you a tour of the unit. Obviously, this is the nurses' station. Anytime you need help or have a question, you can come here. Also, this is where you'll come for your medications."

She turned around. The nurses' station opened out onto a large room with sofas, chairs and a couple of tables. There was a TV mounted on the far wall. Five or six patients were there, reading or watching TV. "This is the common area," she said. 'You can relax here if you don't have a therapy group. We also have mandatory community meetings here twice a day, at eight in the morning and eight in the evening." She showed him two open booths with payphones. "The staff are not responsible for answering these phones. These are for the patients, and if they ring, any nearby patient should answer it and try to locate the patient whose call it is. If you can't find the patient, just take a message and write it on the board here."

Finally she showed him a large marker board on a wall near the nurses' station. "This is very important. You'll see that all the patients' first names and room numbers are here. You'll also see the names of your assigned counselor and nurse. These are changed by shift, but generally we try to keep the assignments the same each day, so you have some continuity. Your counselor is always available if you feel the need to talk, or if you're feeling unsafe. You should see your nurse for medications and any physical issues you might have. Any questions about all this?"

Matthew shook his head.

Next she led him to the dining room and adjoining kitchen. There were about a dozen tables of various sizes. A few patients were sitting at one of the tables, talking and eating snacks. "Meals are brought up three times a day," she said. "The times are noted on the weekly schedule I'll be giving you." She pointed at the kitchen area where there was a refrigerator, a counter with a sink, and lots of cabinets. "You'll find plastic utensils, cookies, crackers, juices and so forth in there. If you save any food, make sure you put your name on it. Otherwise it's fair game." She chuckled. "Even then it's usually fair game."

She led him past the closed doors of some patients' rooms to the end of a hall, and showed him where to get towels and extra blankets, and the laundry room. Finally she led him to his room. There were two beds, two plain armoires which had small desks attached, a bathroom, and a large window which overlooked the approach to the building.

"You don't have a roommate for now, but probably in a day or two someone will join you."

Then she asked him to remove his belt and tie, and to empty his pockets. She took these items, and left the room for a moment. Then she returned with a hospital johnny, some skid-proof socks with rubber spots on the bottom, a toothbrush, toothpaste and a comb. She asked him to go into the bathroom and put on the johnny. When he came out, she handed him a few papers.

"There's a schedule there of all the daily groups, meal times and free time. There's also a list of unit rules, and a menu which you fill out in the evening for the following day's meals. Just leave it at the nurses' station. You'll see a menu basket on the counter."

She told him that if he was hungry now, she could arrange to have a meal brought up for him, but he shook his head. "No, thank you." He had absolutely no appetite. The huge knot in his stomach took care of that.

"Okay then, Matthew. Do you have any questions I can answer for you now?"

"No, I guess not."

"Well, I'm your assigned nurse for the evening, so feel free to find me if you have any questions. Your counselor for the evening is Todd, and you can ask him for help too. The other patients are very helpful, as well."

"Thank you."

"Oh, one more thing," she said. "There's always a nurse or counselor walking around the unit doing what we call 'checks'. Every fifteen or twenty minutes, around the clock, they knock on the door and peek in to see that you're okay. They'll say 'checks'. At night they may shine a flashlight on you. It might be a little disconcerting at first, but after a while you'll get used to it. You might want to leave your door ajar so that it's less disruptive."

He nodded. "Okay." The nurse left, leaving the door slightly ajar. He sat down on the bed. He felt empty, and in a kind of shock. He laid down, but remained wide awake. And just as the nurse had said, every fifteen minutes a nurse or counselor with a clipboard would tap on the door, say "Checks," and look in on him.

As it was nearing nine o'clock, and he was drained, he decided to go to bed. He walked out to the nurse's station and was administered his medications. Then he went back to his room, brushed his teeth and went to bed. He laid there for a long while thinking about all that had happened that day. He kept replaying his long ride on the subway, the writing of the suicide note, the walk in the subway tunnel, and the police and ambulance who'd arrived so quickly. He couldn't believe he was now in a psychiatric hospital, and not dead. Yet, though he was still alive, he nonetheless felt dead. He was dead inside.

The checks continued as he laid in bed, though the staff didn't say anything now, but only peered in with a flashlight. Finally, he drifted off into a fitful sleep. He woke up several times during the night, disoriented for a moment until he remembered where he was. Then he'd sink into sleep again.

At some time during the night he was awakened by the sounds of screaming and shouting outside his door in the common area. He jumped out of bed and opened his door. A young woman was being wrestled to the floor by two staffers, and she was kicking, clawing and screaming. All the doors around the common room opened partway, with patients peering in curiosity at the violence taking place. A security guard and a nurse rushed over. The guard pinned her down roughly, and the nurse inserted a needle into her which sedated her within a matter of seconds. One of the counselors stood up and looked around at all the patients peeking at the action. "Everybody, please close your doors and go back to bed. There's nothing to see here. Go back to bed."

Mathew closed his door, but thought, 'There's nothing to see here? Is he serious? We just saw a fellow human being go insane.' His adrenaline was pumping, as was his empathy and sadness. 'What have I gotten myself into?' He laid down again, and thought about what he'd seen, about what suffering that patient was enduring. In time, out of sheer emotional exhaustion, he drifted back into sleep.

He woke up around seven o'clock, and went to the window. It was a gray, rainy day. It perfectly matched his mood. He thought about the girl who'd flipped out during the night. He wondered what had become of her, where she was now, what she was feeling. He went out to the nurses' station to get his meds, and one of nurses came over. "Good morning, Matthew," she said. "Welcome to the unit. I'm Carla, your nurse for the day."

"Hi, Carla," he said, weakly.

"Did you sleep okay last night?"

"Not really."

"Well, if you're having trouble sleeping, don't suffer all night. Come out to the nurse's station, and if a doctor has cleared you for sleep medications, we can give that to you and it should help."

"Thank you. I'll probably do that." He paused a moment. "What happened to the woman who . . . who freaked out during the night? Is she okay?"

"Yes. She's fine. She's in solitary right now, resting, but she's doing okay."

Matthew nodded.

She asked him to sit, and she took his temperature and blood pressure.

"We'll be having the community meeting in a few minutes in the common area, so you might want to stick around."

"Okay," he said.

He wandered into the common area and sat down. There were some old newspapers and magazines scattered on the small table next to him. There were a few other patients in the room. The TV was on, tuned to a news station. Matthew didn't feel like reading or watching TV, so he just sat there, staring into space. Again he thought about what had happened the day before. He couldn't believe it; it was if he was looking at someone else's experiences, not his own.

Over the next ten minutes, more and more patients filtered into the room, filling the sofas and chairs. He felt self-conscious, as he was one of the few patients dressed in the flimsy hospital johnnies. Everyone else was dressed in sweat suits or jeans or shorts. Altogether, there were about twenty patients. Several of them said hi to him, introduced themselves, and asked him his name. He noticed right away that most of the patients were woman, ranging from their teens to middle age. The few males were also in that age group. He learned later that there was a separate unit for elderly patients. At eight o'clock one of the counselors appeared, a large, muscular African-American with close-cropped hair and a goatee. He radiated a kind of positive energy. He turned off the TV and asked one of the patients nearest the phones to take them off their hooks.

The patients were arranged roughly in a circle, and the counselor took a seat as part of the circle. He scanned the group for a moment, and asked if there were any new patients. A middle-aged woman tentatively raised her hand, and Matthew followed suit.

"Well, welcome," he said. "I'm Randy, as most of you know, "and this is our community meeting. What we do is we go around the room, give our first names, and then set some personal goals for the day. They don't have to be earth-shaking; they might be as simple as meeting with your counselor and doctor, and trying to attend your assigned groups. After that, we open the floor to any issues that patients would like to bring to our attention, such as complaints about the food," and at that he smiled, and several patients chuckled, "or people who are leaving their clothes in the washer or dryer long after they're done. Pretty much anything you want to bring to the attention of the staff or the other patients."

Matthew nodded.

"Oh, I almost forgot," Randy said. "Are any of you being discharged today?"

A teenaged boy raised his hand.

"Robbie," Randy said. "Good for you. When are you leaving?"

"I'm supposed to meet with my doctor at eleven, and then as soon as the paperwork is done, I'll be leaving. Around noon, I guess."

"Well that's wonderful," Randy said. "Is there anything you'd like to say to the rest of the group before you leave?"

Robbie looked around the room. "I guess I'd just like to say thank you to everyone who helped me, or tried to help me, since I've been here. I feel much better now than when I came here, and a lot of you helped me a lot." He paused for a moment. "I'll miss you guys."

Most of the patients nodded, and said "Good luck, Robbie," or "We'll miss you too."

Randy said, "Yes. Good luck to you Robbie. We all hope that you never have to come back here again," and he smiled.

Robbie smiled as well. "Yeah, me too," he said.

"Okay," Randy said. He turned to the girl sitting next to him. "Vickie, we'll start with you."

Vickie looked to be about twenty years old, anorexic, and very depressed. She kept her eyes focused on the floor and spoke slowly and quietly. "Well, as he just said, I'm Vickie." She paused for a moment. "I guess my goal for the day is just to get through it. Try to stay out of bed, try to eat, and maybe go to a group or two."

Randi nodded. "Thank you, Vickie."

And so it went, around the room. As Matthew waited with increasing anxiety for his turn, he looked around at the other patients. Every degree of emotional expression was present. Some of the patients looked messy, dull-eyed and almost catatonic. Others, presumably closer to a discharge, looked bright eyed, and tended to smile and be engaged in the group.

Finally it was Matthew's turn to speak. "My name is Matthew," he said. "I just came in last night. I'm not sure what my goal is . . . maybe to meet with my counselor and go to my assigned groups."

"Well, again, welcome," Randy said. "Don't hesitate to ask any of the staff, or other patients, if you have any questions."

"Thank you," Matthew said. He felt relieved when they moved on to the patient beside him.

After they'd gone around the circle, and a few complaints were registered, Randi thanked everyone, and announced that breakfast would be up in about ten minutes.

Matthew actually had a slight appetite now, and he followed the other patients into the dining room. A few minutes later a large, multi-shelved cart was rolled in, loaded with trays and a slip of paper denoting the name of the patient. Matthew found one with his name on it, but as he'd arrive too late the previous evening to get his menu in on time, he was given a generic breakfast of scrambled eggs, bacon, toast and orange juice. He carried his tray to a small, empty table in the corner. He didn't feel like sitting at one of the large tables where the more animated and healthier patients were sitting. He wanted to eat alone. But as the tables filled up, an older man approached and asked if he could join him. Matthew nodded, and the man placed his tray on the table and sat down. "I'm Joseph," he said.

"Matthew," he replied. Matthew really did not feel like talking, and he was relieved that Joseph didn't seem to want talk either. The two of them ate their food in silence, mostly keeping their eyes lowered and focused on their plates. After a time, Matthew began to appreciate this. Unlike the world outside the hospital, no one here expected you to be social. You could sit at a table across from another person and never utter a word, and that was okay. You didn't have to utter a word of small talk. Matthew was amazed at this. It felt honest and pure, people acting as they felt, rather than as they were expected to act.

When he'd finished breakfast, Matthew went back to his room and checked his schedule. He was slated for several therapy groups, and he decided he would try to attend all of them. By the end of the day, he was feeling considerably better than he had that morning. He had participated in the groups, and felt that he'd made a positive impression on the other patients and counselors. A hint of his previous ambition seemed to be stirring, but in this case it was to be a model patient. His counselor for the day, Gabe, had checked in with him a few times, and he felt comfortable talking to him. One thing Matthew had asked was why virtually everyone on the unit was wearing street clothes, while he was stuck with a johnny. Gabe explained that the flight, or escape, risk was much higher for new patients, but that after a couple of days his clothes would be returned, except for any belts or ties.

"What about shaving?" Matthew had asked.

"Just go to the nurses' station and ask. They'll give you a razor if you're feeling safe, but for obvious reasons they'll have to be with you while you shave."

That afternoon, Matthew phoned Helen and told her what he'd done, and that he was now at McLean. There was a long silence before she responded.

"Would you like to see the boys?"

"Yes. Very much. Please. Visiting hours are four till six."

"I'll bring them over."

"Thank you, Helen."

She hung up.

Matthew felt the long-forgotten sensation of joy. He couldn't wait to see the boys.

Around five o'clock, Gabe came in and told him that his wife and sons were here, and would he like to see them. "Yes. Very much," he replied.

A moment later Helen and the boys entered his room. He glanced at Helen for a moment, and seeing the coldness in her eyes, he looked at the boys and smiled. "Hey, guys!"

They came over to him as he sat on the edge of the bed, and he hugged both of them at the same time. He felt his eyes welling, but told himself he was not going to cry. He talked to the boys for a while, then decided he wanted to speak to Helen in private, so he led the boys out to the common area, where there was a table with paper and crayons, and asked them to draw some pictures for a while he and Mom talked for a bit. He went back into the room, and left the door open so he could keep an eye on the boys.

"Thank you for bringing them over," he said.

"Why did you do it?" she asked, her arms crossed.

He hung his head. "I . . . I'm sick. I'm sick in the head. They tell me I have clinical depression.

"Do you realize how much it would hurt the boys if you killed yourself? You of all people ought to understand that."

He looked up at her. "I know. It was a mistake. A bad one. I'm just not in my right mind right now."

"You haven't been in your right mind for quite a while. And whatever the cause is, you've been acting like you're the only person in the world. Your selfishness has exceeded all bounds."

Matthew hung his head again and started to cry. "I'm sorry . . . I'm so sorry."

Neither of them spoke for a time. Finally Michael came into the room, and Matthew wiped his eyes. "Hey, Buddy." Justin followed his brother into the room. "It's so good to see you, you little men." He smiled and hugged them both again.

He played with the boys for a few minutes while Helen lingered by the door. "Okay, boys," she said. "Time to go. Say goodbye to Daddy."

Matthew hung his head, then looked at her. "I'll walk you to the door."

They walked through the common area, and as they approached the nurses' station Matthew asked the nurse if she would let them out. The nurse nodded and walked with them to the locked double doors. She unlocked the door, and Matthew knelt down to hug the boys again and say goodbye. Justin started to cry, and Helen picked him up. Helen and the boys passed through the doorway, and the door closed and locked. Through the small window in the door, Matthew saw Justin reaching toward the window, calling for Daddy and starting to cry. Matthew's pain became unbearable, and he sank down onto the floor, has back against the door. He began sobbing uncontrollably. He wanted so badly to be dead.

After a few minutes he went back to his room and laid down in bed, curling into a fetal position. In time, he began to feel a little better as he thought about his boys, about how nice it had been to see them. He even smiled. After an hour, he went out into the common area and watched some TV and talked to a few of the patients. His mood improved. He'd been knocked down hard, but he felt safe. He couldn't harm himself. And despite the pain of their departure, he felt happy to have seen the boys, the only joys in his life. He was grateful.

As he laid in bed that night, he felt better than he'd felt the night before. He had gotten to see and hug his boys. And he was beginning to adapt to his new surroundings. He felt relieved at the thought that he had nothing to do here but try to get better. No responsibilities, no pressure—just the goal of getting better. He'd even struck up some conversations with a few of the other patients. He was beginning to feel like a member of the unit, rather than the wasted outcast he'd felt like the day before. He was still deeply depressed, but he was among his own kind here.

The following day he was pleased to have his clothes returned to him. He felt less self-conscious now.

In the afternoon he returned from a group to find a roommate sitting in the room. Matthew introduced himself. They exchanged a few pleasantries. His name was Joshua, and he was an obviously depressed man about Matthew's age. He was soft spoken, and very neat in appearance, despite the johnny. Matthew told him it wasn't a bad place, that the staff were kind and really wanted to help people, as did the fellow patients.

Joshua nodded, but didn't pick up the threads of the conversation after that. He simply pulled the blanket and sheets off his bed and proceeded to re-make it with military precision, his back to Mathew.

Over the next day or two Matthew was able to talk to him a bit more, and Joshua's mood seemed to improve slightly when his clothes were returned. His father had apparently come by and left him several changes of clothes.

Matthew soon noticed that Joshua folded and refolded his clothes until they were meticulously shaped, then carefully placed them in his drawers or closet, sometimes taking them out several times until they were exactly the way he wanted them. He watched as Joshua positioned his slippers parallel to the lines of the floor tiles, stood before them, and with a deep breath and the utmost care, stepped forward into them. Then he walked to the closed door, placed his hand on the handle, took another deep breath, and opened the door. He stood there for a moment, looked around the door frame, then crossed the threshold as if he were stepping into a minefield. Matthew suddenly understood what it meant to have obsessive compulsive disorder. He felt bad for Joshua.

One time as Matthew laid on his bed, reading, Joshua came into the room. He took his slippers off and placed them neatly on the floor, perfectly parallel to the tiles. Then he proceeded to tear his neatly made bed apart, and remake it with excruciating deliverance. Matthew watched all this with a mixture of fascination and pity. "Joshua," he said, at last. "I'd like to ask you to do something for me, as a favor."

Joshua looked at him warily.

"I'd like you to pick up your slippers."

"Pick up my slippers?"

"Yes. Pick up your slippers."

Joshua looked puzzled, but he picked up the slippers.

"Okay," Matthew said. "Now I want you to drop them on the floor."

"Drop them on the floor?"

"Yes."

Joshua dropped them on the floor, and they landed at odd angles to each other and the lines between the floor tiles. He bent as if to arrange them.

"No, don't touch them," Matthew said. Joshua stood up looked at Matthew. "Okay. Now I want you to step into them just as they are. No arranging them. Just stick your foot into them just as they are."

Joshua looked troubled.

"You can do this, "Matthew said.

Joshua stood before the slippers lying at odd angles, took a deep breath, and stepped into them.

"You did it!" Matthew exclaimed. "You scored a victory over your OCD!"

Joshua looked at Matthew with an intensely serious expression. "Do you think I did? Do you really think I did?"

"Hell, yes!"

"You know," Joshua said. "My mother doesn't think I have OCD. What do you think, Matthew?"

"Joshua, I've been watching you for several days now, watching you fold and re-fold your clothes, watching you make and re-make your bed even though it's already tight as a drum, watching your rituals with your slippers and going out the door, and I have to say if anybody has OCD, it's you."

"That's what all my doctors say, but my mother doesn't agree. Why would she say that?"

"I don't know, Joshua. Maybe she just can't accept that her son has a mental illness. Maybe she's in some sort of denial."

"Because my dad, who is divorced from my mom, thinks I do have it. You know, OCD."

"Well, I agree with your father and your doctors. You definitely have OCD. There's no doubt about it."

"Do you really think so?"

"Yes, I really do. But it's nothing to be ashamed of, Joshua. It's a disease, just like depression or cancer. It's a disease, and can be treated with medications, and hard work on your part."

A look of consternation came over Joshua's face. "But what should I tell my mother?"

"The truth. You should tell her that the medical experts are clear that you have obsessive compulsive disorder. Again, it's nothing to be ashamed of, Joshua. It's an illness, not a weakness."

Joshua stood there looking at him, and gave a slide nod.

"Okay, Joshua. You did great with the slippers. Now I want you to do something else."

A look of fear came over Joshua. "What do you want me to do?"

"I want you to walk out of this room without any ritual."

Joshua looked puzzled. "What do you mean?"

"I mean, I want you to walk up to that door, and without any hesitation, open it up and step out into the hall. I don't want you to line up your feet, I don't want you to look around the door frame as if to ascertain if it's wide enough—because it's plenty wide enough—and I don't want you taking a deep breath, like you're about to jump into deep water. I want you to just walk up, open the door, and go out. You can do this. I know you can."

"Do you really think so?"

"Yes, I do. I think you can do this, Joshua. So do it, right now."

Joshua took a deep breath and walked to the door. He looked back at Matthew, and Matthew gave a smile and a nod. "You can do this."

Joshua placed his hand on the door knob and pulled the door open. Then, without hesitating, he stepped out into the hall. He turned and gave Matthew a big grin. "I did it!"

Matthew grinned back at him. "You're damn right you did, Joshua. You can whip this thing!"

"Do you really think so?"

"Yes, I do. If you're willing to work at it."

Joshua smiled, then walked away. Matthew smiled to himself. He'd done something good to help one of his fellow patients. If only, he thought, they could help him.

When Joshua returned later on, Matthew said, "We're going to do one more thing for today, okay, Joshua?"

Once again Joshua looked worried. "I'll try."

"Okay. What I'd like you to do first is open one of your drawers, take the clothes out and put them on the bed."

Joshua did as he was asked. Then he looked at Matthew again.

"Now, I want you unfold them and just loosely pile them up."

Again, Joshua followed Matthew's instructions.

"Okay, Joshua. Here's the hard part. I want you to just take the pile and drop it in the drawer, just like it is. No arranging."

Joshua looked at the pile and then at Matthew. "I can't do that."

"Sure you can. It's a matter of willpower."

Joshua shook his head. "I just can't do that, Matthew."

"Why not?"

"Because I have OCD."

"Yes, I understand that. But you saw earlier that you can get over that roadblock if you really try. It's mind over matter, Joshua. Your mind over that pile of clothes."

"I'm sorry. I just can't do that." He hung his head for a moment, then turned and started folding his clothes.

Matthew felt a mix of pity and frustration. He couldn't bear to watch him fold and arrange his clothes, so he left the room and sat with his book in the common area.

Matthew attended a few therapy groups after lunch that day, then, during break, went to his room to read. As he approached his room, he saw Joshua inspecting the doorway, then stepping through as if he'd just avoided some great danger. Matthew was disappointed to see this. He greeted him in passing, and went into the room. The first thing he noticed were Joshua's slippers arranged neatly on the floor, perfectly in parallel with the tiles. Then he noticed the skin-tight bed covers. He was crestfallen. It was as if Joshua had completely forgotten what he'd achieved earlier in the day. He laid down on his own bed and opened a book, but he couldn't read because he kept thinking of Joshua. He wondered if Joshua would ever be cured, not only of his OCD, but the depression that it obviously fueled. Josh knew he had a problem, but he seemed completely powerless to do anything about it. He was trapped in his mad, OCD world. Matthew felt a rising wave of sadness and empathy for this poor, gentle and intelligent soul who seemed doomed to such a world. How could God, if he exists, do this to Joshua? He sighed deeply, and laid there for a long time, finally closing the book. He felt that he'd in some sad way closed the book on Joshua as well. It made him want to cry. In time, he drifted off to sleep.

Later, he woke and heard Joshua come into the room. He had a strange, disturbed look on his face.

Matthew sat up. "Joshua, are you okay?"

"I don't know," he replied.

"Well, tell me. Did something happen?"

"Sort of, but I'm not really sure."

"What happened?"

"Well, I was in my therapist's office, and I was talking on the speaker phone with my mother. And I guess I started talking to her like a baby."

"I don't understand."

"I mean, I wasn't speaking words. I was just kind of making gibberish noises in a high voice, like a baby."

Matthew was appalled. "What did she say?"

"She got very upset and said it was a cruel joke, and demanded that the therapist explain what was going on."

"And what did he say?"

"He told her that he didn't think it was a joke at all; that I was sliding into some kind of psychosis possibly unrelated to my OCD—which, as I told you—she doesn't even believe I have."

"And why did you start talking like a baby to your mother?"

"I'm not really sure. But babies are pure and innocent, aren't they?" Joshua looked into Matthew's eyes as if looking for salvation.

Matthew was silent for a moment. He was deeply upset and saddened by what he'd just heard. "Yes, Joshua. Babies are innocent," was all he could muster. He was devastated. Then he got up and walked out of the room, unable to bear the tragedy of his roommate.

The following day Joshua was transferred to another unit. He carefully packed his things, then shook Matthew's hand and thanked him for trying to help. "I'm sorry I disappointed you," he said.

"Joshua," he replied, "please don't think of it that way. You need help, and you're going to get it. Forget what your mother says. She is completely out of touch with you. You take care of yourself, okay?"

"I will," he said, and he left the room. Matthew thought about Joshua for a long while. Then a more practical consideration entered his thoughts: how long would he have the pleasure of having the whole room to himself? He didn't have to wait long to find out. Matthew returned to his room after dinner and found a new roommate. He introduced himself. He knew after a few moments of conversation that this man was on a plane of his own.

His name was Gerhardt, German-born, and he was utterly and completely different from Joshua. Gerhardt was short and muscular, bold and loud, and told Matthew that he, Gerhardt, was God. Or rather, a manifestation of God, as was Jesus. And he'd draped a German flag over his bed.

Their first night together, after they'd been sent to their rooms, Matthew asked what had brought him to McLean.

"I took a taxi from Vermont to Boston—to Logan Airport—and I became fixated on a luggage sticker that was on the floor."

Matthew didn't even know how to respond to such a bizarre act, other that feeling sad.

He decided to probe a bit to find out who this guy was, and why he thought he was God.

"Gerhardt, let me ask you this. When you say you are God, do you mean you alone are God? Or do you mean that God is in all people, so that I could say, like you, 'I am God.' Am I God just the way you are God?"

Gerhardt didn't respond for a moment. "That's a good question," he replied. There was another long pause. "I think that you are God, but in a different way. You're God the same way that animals, plants and rocks are God. The way that the entire universe is God. You're sort of like the body of God. But me, I'm more than God's body. I'm also God's soul. I share God's light, in fact I am God's light, whereas you and the rest of the world are . . . are reflections of God's light. So you, Matthew, are Godly, whereas I am God himself. Can you understand that?"

"I understand what it is you are saying, though I can't say I agree. You believe that you are the incarnation of God, like Jesus?"

"Yes. I am the incarnation of God, and that's the difference between you and me."

"But Jesus was the incarnation of God, God's only son. Are you the second coming of Christ?" Matthew was enjoying this. He was fascinated by the world according to Gerhardt.

"No. I'm not Jesus." He paused. "I'm like his brother."

"You're his brother? His younger brother?"

"In a divine way, yes. But I am God, too, just as Jesus was."

"Okay. But Jesus came to save mankind, to die for our sins so that we would be redeemed. So, what are you here for, Gerhardt?"

"I have more than one mission. In fact, I have lots of missions." He walked to the window and stood there for a moment, silent.

"Can you share with me some of your missions?" Matthew asked.

Gerhardt turned around. "I can share some of them, but not all. Some of them mankind is not yet ready to know or hear."

"What can you share with me now?"

"Well, one of my missions is to save the Jews."

Matthew arched his brows. "To save the Jews? Save them from what?"

"From themselves."

"I don't understand," Matthew said.

"The Jews have never accepted God's truth, my truth. But, even worse, they have taken false idols: mammon, and Zionism. And the ones who haven't are so caught up in the Talmud and the Zohar—on what they can or cannot eat; on what time of the day they can or cannot fold laundry or take a shit... their heads are so far up their asses that they can't see God. They're all running around selling shares in Holocaust, Incorporated, or controlling the media or the financial markets or U.S. policy. The *Protocols of Zion* may be a hoax, but that doesn't make them any less true. The Jews are destroying the Earth, and I'm here—among many other reasons—to convince them that they need to change their ways, or they're doomed. They think because they are God's so-called Chosen People, that they are superior to everyone else. They're all for multi-culturalism and gay rights except when it comes to Jews. They're just as racist as the Nazis."

"So what are you saying, that the Jews need to become Christians or be exterminated?"

"No, I wouldn't exterminate them, because they are still God's children. But you, and all the other gentiles, will exterminate them, once you realize that the Jews have been robbing you blind and manipulating the government and the media. So, one of the reasons I'm here is to save the Jews from you."

There was a pause. "So, how exactly do you plan to do all this?"

"Very slowly," Gerhardt replied.

Matthew almost laughed.

"But I have time, lots of time," Gerhardt said. "It may take centuries, but I will be here, in one form or another, to make it happen."

"So tell me. Besides saving the Jews, what's another mission you have?"
"Well, one is the public drinking water."
"The public drinking water?"
"Yes. Governments around the world, in collusion, are poisoning the water supply with special chemicals that make people docile and compliant. It's a huge plot."

Matthew was amazed and saddened by how far out of touch with reality Gerhardt was.

Gerhard was now striding back and forth across the room. "Have you noticed that countries where the water supply and water treatment are controlled by the government, that those countries are the most stable? It's pure mind control. Countries that don't have this control—the people are out demonstrating in the streets by the hundreds of thousands, the millions, seeking to overthrow their governments, and this is because their governments haven't yet been able to poison their minds. It's all about control, pure and simple."

Matthew shook his head. He decided to go on the offensive. "Gerhardt, I know you don't want to hear this, but all this stuff about you and God and the Jews and the water supply—it's all nonsense. All these things are just figments of your imagination. They're one of the reasons you're in this hospital."

Gerhardt whirled and stared at Matthew with a look approaching hatred. "Get thee behind me, Satan!"

And for the two days that Matthew and he continued to share a room, Gerhardt wouldn't speak to, or even look at, Matthew. Matthew regretted what he'd said, and tried to apologize, but Gerhardt ignored him. Two days later he flipped out in the common room, screaming and throwing punches at the staff. He was sedated, placed on a stretcher with four-point restraints, and taken to another unit. Matthew wondered what would become of him, and it saddened him.

That evening Matthew was perusing the donated books—mostly romance and detective novels—in the small bookcase in the common room, and was surprised to find Jean-Paul Sartre's novel, *Nausea*. A book with such a title appealed to him, and though he'd never read it, he'd heard of it and knew that it was a grim novel of existential philosophy. He wondered why the staff would allow such a book to be in the unit's bookcase, but figured that with it being so thin, and perhaps unfamiliar to staff, it slipped through. He started reading it right away, and found that the dark, godless world of Antoine Roquentin mirrored his own. It whetted his thirst for more, and he decided that when he was discharged he would read more about existentialist philosophy.

One day Matthew saw on the unit schedule that there was a creative writing group scheduled for that afternoon, and decided to attend. The group met three times a week. It was led by an attractive dark-haired, dark-eyed nurse who looked like anything but a nurse, and more like a gypsy. But he liked her energy and the sort of artistic flair she exuded, which was reflected in her beads, flamboyant earrings and colorful, almost sexy, clothing. There were eight people in the group. They all looked at her expectantly.

"Hi. For those of you who don't know me, though most of you do, my name's Moira. Today I'm giving you all a homework assignment," she said, looking around the table. "I want you all to think of some episode in your life—it could be recent, or it could be from your childhood—and write about it. But I don't want you to write about it in the first person. Do you understand what I mean by that?" Without waiting for a response, she continued. "The first person is when you use 'I' as the narrator. As in 'I did this, and then I did that.' I want you to use the third person view instead. So instead of saying, 'I did this, or he did this to me,' I want you to say, 'she did this or he did that'; in other words, I want you to write about your experience as if you were someone else watching you, and describing what he or she saw. As if you are telling a story about someone else, only the story is really about you. Do you understand what I am saying?" She looked around the table, and everyone was nodding. "Good," she said. "And don't worry about trying to write a masterpiece, and don't worry if it's only a few paragraphs. I just want you to think of something that affected you deeply, whether in a good way or a bad way. Again, don't worry about whether it's 'good writing'. Just get something down on paper. And hey, if nothing comes; if you just can't do it, or if it's too upsetting, that's okay too. You don't have to do this. But I'd like you all to give it a try."

One patient spoke up. "Why the third person?"

"Good question. The reason I ask for the third person is that I've found, over years of doing this, that patients are often able to write more freely about an experience that deeply affected them if they can step back from it, view it from a distance, as if it was happening to someone else, rather than themselves, even though it is themselves that they are writing about. Do you understand what I'm saying? Does that make sense?"

The patient nodded.

"Good," she said. "Okay. I want you to use the rest of this session thinking about the event you'd like to write about, and if you feel like getting started on it, to start writing about it, feel free. There's plenty of paper here on the table, and pens. Give it a shot. I think you'll find this a very interesting and meaningful assignment. I'd like you to have them done by the Wednesday session, okay? Okay. Go to it. Oh, and if you'd rather go back to your rooms to start this, that's fine. Or if you'd like to stay here for the rest of the hour, that's fine too. Whatever's comfortable for you."

Matthew thought for a moment, then excused himself to go to his room. When he got there, he sat at the desk for a long time, deep in thought. Perhaps because his birthday was tomorrow, a memory of a childhood birthday came to mind. That's it, he thought. That's what I'm going to write about. And without hesitation, he started writing. It flowed from his memory to the paper almost without effort. Once he started, he couldn't stop, and in an hour it was done.

*The Birthday Party
Matthew St. Clare*

Matthew's eighth birthday was memorable—indeed, he never forgot it. But it was not a happy memory. Certainly, the beginning of the day had been happy, with his mother hugging him and treating the birthday boy like a little prince. But that part of the day Matthew doesn't remember very well. It's what happened later that he remembered so clearly.

Matthew and his mother, who had recently lost father and husband by suicide, had moved into an apartment on the second floor of a two-story house a few months later. There were a number of young kids in the neighborhood, and though Matthew had been shy about making new friends, and in fact had come home crying on more than one occasion, having been picked on by some of the kids, Matthew thought that in recent weeks he was beginning to fit in. A few of the kids had become friendly, and he felt that he was becoming just another kid in the neighborhood, instead of the new kid, the stranger, on the block.

So, a few weeks before his birthday, his mother decided to have a birthday party for him and invite the kids from the neighborhood. She bought a pack of festive birthday cards, and helped him write them out, with Matthew supplying the names. The next morning they walked through the neighborhood and put the invitations in the mailboxes where the boys lived.

As the day drew close, Matthew became more and more excited, partly because of the thrill of opening presents, and partly because of the party itself. His mother was excited too, and she was having fun planning activities, such as pin-the-tail on the donkey, bobbing for apples, and ideas for a piñata they would make together.

The piñata became a pet project for both of them, and they worked on it for a couple of days. His mother made a special paste, and with cardboard and newspaper, they fashioned a big donkey. She'd bought bags of candy and a bunch of little toys—Silly Putty, green army men, packs of baseball cards; all kinds of things—and they stuffed them into the donkey, along with lots of quarters and even a few dollar bills. Then they painted it with thick colors. It looked great, and Matthew could hardly wait to take a whack at it. There were things in there he really wanted.

Finally the big day arrived. It was a Saturday. Matthew was now eight, and feeling more like the "Little Man" his mother often called him. He couldn't wait till the party, which was at one o'clock. He was dying to open presents, and to see who would finally crack open the piñata, followed by the mad rush to gather up the goodies that would shower down. The apartment was filled with the smell of the cake his mother had baked, and though she wouldn't let him see it when she was finishing it, he knew it would be chocolate, with chocolate frosting, because that was his favorite. He especially liked the creamy frosting.

His mother had put up all sorts of decorations—crepe ribbons, balloons, and a special birthday tablecloth with matching napkins. At one point that morning she came over to him, cupped his face in her hands, kissed him, and said "This is the exact time of day, Sweetheart, that you were born. 11:35. Now you are officially eight years old. I love you, Matthew." Then she kissed him and drew him close, and hugged him. He hugged her back, and said, "I love you too, Mom."

At noon, an hour before the party, everything was ready. The next hour was one of the longest in Matthew's short life. He just couldn't wait. The clock on the kitchen wall seemed to have slowed down, almost to a stop. He watched the second hand move, then stop, move, then stop. It was unbearable. His mother grinned at him every time he came in to look at the clock.

At about ten before one, crazy with anticipation and not knowing else to do, Matthew went into the parlor and stood at the window, staring down at the front walkway in case anyone was early. Every couple of minutes he'd go back to the kitchen and look at the clock, which seemed to be moving even slower, just to torture him. Then, back to the window.

Eventually, one o'clock came and went. Five past, ten past, twenty past, and still no one had shown up. Matthew was a bit confused as he stood at the window looking up and down the street. He went into the kitchen and noticed something different about his mother's expression. She was still smiling at him, but her eyes didn't look right, they didn't match her smile. "When are they coming?" he asked.

"They're probably just running a little bit late, Honey. They'll be here soon."

He went back to the window. At last, at 1:30, he saw one of the kids, Robbie, coming up the street on his bike. He rode right by without looking and disappeared down the street and around the corner. Matthew felt something really unpleasant, and his eyes blurred with tears.

He went into the kitchen, where his mother was now sitting at the table, smoking a cigarette. "Mom, I just saw Robbie ride by on his bike. But we invited him to the party. I know it. Did we put the right time on the invitations?"

His mother pulled him over, hugged him, and burst into tears. "I love you, Baby," she said. "You're the best boy any mother could ever want. Better than any of those other kids."

Matthew would always remember that moment, for he realized at that moment that no one was coming to his birthday party, that his mother was broken-hearted, that he was broken-hearted, and that he would have to hide it from her and be strong for her, because he was now indeed the little man of the house. In fact, the only man.

He went back into the parlor, but didn't look out the window. He looked around at all the decorations. His mom had made it all look so nice and festive, and now it just looked sad. He looked at the piñata, standing in the corner. His felt the tears coming again. He walked down the hall to his bedroom and quietly closed the door.

Later that day, he saw Moira at the nurses' station, and handed her the story. "I finished it," he said. She looked at him with some surprise. "That's wonderful, Matthew. I'll be sure to read it before our next meeting."

"Thank you."

"I look forward to it," she said, and then she turned and went into the nurse's station.

Matthew went back to his room and laid down. He thought about what he'd written, or more accurately, the event about which he'd written. When he'd been writing about it, it didn't really bother him. Perhaps it was the third person view that had protected him. But now, as he laid there thinking about it, it bothered him. In fact, it more than bothered him. It made him very sad, and tears welled in his eyes. But then he admonished himself for indulging in self pity.

The next day, as he was reading in the common room, Moira came up to him. "Matthew," she said. "I read your work last night. It's so beautiful. Sad, but so beautifully written. It made me cry."

"Yeah, well it made me cry too. But thank you for your kind words."

"I'd like you to share it with the group tomorrow. Is that okay with you?"

He shrugged. "Sure, that's fine with me."

"Great," she said, handing it back to him. "That's wonderful. See you tomorrow, okay?"

He nodded. "Yes. See you tomorrow."

As she walked away, Matthew allowed himself a small smile. He was proud of what he'd written, and flattered that Moira had liked it so much and wanted to share it with the group.

The following day he was very much looking forward to the group. As the patients sat around the long table, Moira came in, in another of her sexy gypsy outfits. "Okay," she said. "Do we have any newcomers here today?" No one raised their hand or spoke up. "Good," she said. "Okay, how many of you completed the homework assignment I gave on Monday?" Most of the patients raised their hands. "Great," she said. "And if you didn't, that's okay. Those of you who did, hang on to them, because I'd like to ask each of you to read them, or at least part of them, if they're more than a few pages, so that we can hear what you had to say and maybe talk about it, if you're comfortable with that."

"Okay," she said. "Let me ask you this first. Did any of you find the experience helpful in connecting to an experience, good or bad, that you've had?" Most of the patients nodded their heads.

"And did you find writing in the third person a help? Did it help you gain a different perspective?"

Again, most of the patients nodded.

"Excellent," she said. "Well, to get things started, I'd like you, Matthew, to read for us the beautiful piece you wrote about your eighth birthday. Perhaps we can talk about it afterwards, to get people's impressions."

Matthew was flattered. He was proud of what he'd written.

He read it to the group, and when he finished, several of the group members nodded and said things like, "that's sad," or, "that was powerful." One woman said, "I felt so bad for the little boy, for Matthew, and for his mom, too."

Moira looked at Matthew. "Can you tell us why you chose that particular event to write about?"

"Well," he said, "my birthday was yesterday, and I guess it just reminded me of that birthday when I was a kid."

"Well, we all belatedly wish you a happy birthday, Matthew. I'm sorry you had to celebrate it in the hospital."

"Thank you."

"And did that episode influence you, or did you come to any realizations while writing about it?"

He thought for a moment "I think," he began, "that this episode brought me face to face with the realization that I was an outsider, a loner, and that I would always be one. And that a loving parent can't really do anything about it. It was like a little death. And I think it resonates with me today because my illness has made me feel like an outsider—abnormal even—and like then, I am a still a lonely person. Even though I've tried so hard to fit in, to belong, I really am still a lonely outsider."

Moira just looked at Matthew, but didn't say anything. Several of the patients were nodding, as if what he'd said resonated in their own lives.

Moira was still looking at Matthew. "Well," she said, "your answer was as powerful as the piece. Thank you, Matthew."

Moira invited comments from the group, and several patients volunteered comments. They were all of a positive sort, and Matthew simply nodded and thanked each of them when they were done.

At the end of the session, Moira gave them another assignment.

"Okay," she said. "How many of you have ever written poetry?" The patients looked around at each other, and a few of them raised their hands. She pointed at one of the women and said, "Sheila. Tell me, do you write a lot?"

"Actually," she replied, "I keep a journal, and I write poems in it almost every day. In fact, some of the entries are just written as poems."

"That's wonderful," Moira said.

"What about you, Matthew. I saw your hand up."

"Well, when I was in college I was first introduced to the beauty of poetry, thanks to a great professor, and for a while I was writing a lot of poetry. But I haven't really written anything since then, so it's been a dozen or so years since I've written."

Moira nodded. "Well, I'm going to hand out a packet of poems, which I'd like you all to read. They're by various poets, some of them living, and some of them long gone. Read them, and then what I'd like you to do is write a poem about something from your own life. Don't worry about making them rhyme—you'll notice that many of the poems in the packet don't rhyme, they're written in free verse. But they're still poems because they zero in on very powerful experiences and emotions, and are condensed into relatively few words. I'd like all of you to again take an important experience, a moment even, from your lives, and write a poem about it. Again, don't worry about trying to create a masterpiece, or something very long. It can be half a page. This is a creative writing class in a hospital, okay? It's not Harvard, and nobody's getting graded. Just do what you can, and if you can't do it, that's okay. It's strictly voluntary, and I don't want anybody stressing out about it. You've got enough to deal with as it is. Just give it a try, that's all I'm asking. Any questions?"

Nobody responded.

"Okay. Go to it. I'll see you on Friday."

The patients shuffled out of the room, back to their own rooms or the common room. Matthew was excited about the new project. He hadn't written a poem in years, and he was eager to try his hand. Plus, he was developing a crush on Moira, and he wanted to impress her with his writing. So he went back to his room and sat thinking, as he'd done the other night, and a topic eventually floated to the surface of his thoughts. And when it did, he knew instantly that it was his topic. No question about it. He was going to write about his father's suicide. And as he announced this to himself, he felt a tightness in his gut. This was going to be difficult. He decided not to write anything without giving it some serious thought before-hand. He made the painful decision to replay in his mind what had happened or really, just what he'd seen. His father's suicide was always with him, but he very rarely replayed the experience in his mind; in fact, he's always avoided it. And now, he was going to face it square, and write a poem about it. He was afraid, but excited at the same time. He wondered what was going flow out of his pen. When he felt ready, he opened his notebook, picked up a pen, and started writing. He couldn't think of a title, so he launched right into it. He ended it with a quote from somewhere that he'd jotted in his notebook.

> *This is the scene that will not die:*
> *in the cellar, as a young boy, I find my father*
> *hanging from a pipe. I wrap my arms*
> *around his legs and try to lift*
> *to keep the weight off the rope.*
> *He is too heavy, and I am too late,*
> *but I cannot let go. I remember*
> *the roughness of his wool pants*
> *against my wet cheeks.*
> *I tried hard for many years*
> *to understand this act, and failed.*
> *The memory of it comes back*
> *like a streak of lightening, over and over,*
> *illuminating a lifetime of pain.*
> *My family never talked about it.*
> *It was as if it had never happened.*
> *But for me it was happening all the time.*
> *Finally, I'd had enough.*
> *It was about that time that I started*
> *to think about drilling holes in my head.*

Once again he sought out Moira out on the unit, and found her. "Moira," he said. "Once again I guess I'm a little early," and he held the poem out to her.

"Geez, that was fast!" She took the paper and read it right then and there. When she finished, she stared at the paper for a moment. Then she looked up at him. "I don't know what to say, Matthew. It's . . . it's so sad, but so beautifully written. You just wrote this since the end of the group a while ago?"

Matthew nodded. "It just came out," he said. "I only scribbled out or changed a few lines."

"Well, you're really very talented. I'd like you to read this to the group on Friday."

"I'd be happy to."

"Can I keep this till our next group? I'd like to show this to a couple of people."

"Sure, that's fine." He was quite flattered.

"Thank you," she said. "I'll see you around." She turned and walked down the hall. Matthew watched her, her trim, shapely figure, her long curly hair. He watched her till she turned the corner.

Matthew couldn't wait till the Friday group meeting, partly because of his poem, and partly because of her.

On Friday the patients in the group shuffled into the meeting room and took their places around the table. Moira was already there, and she looked as funky and attractive as ever. When everyone had taken their seats, Moira looked around the table and saw that everyone had a sheet, or sheets, of paper in front of them. "That's good," she said. "I see everyone was able to do their homework. That's wonderful."

One middle-aged woman raised her hand.

Moira nodded at her. "Yes, Martha?"

"I don't want to read my poem to the group. Is that okay?"

"That's fine, Martha. No one in this room has to share their poem, if they don't want. This isn't school, here. What I might suggest, though, Martha, is that—if your poem is about something that's really upsetting to you, you might want to go to one of the counselors, or your assigned doctor, to talk about it. It might help you."

Martha nodded.

"Okay," Moira said. "Since Matthew here handed me his assignment about an hour after our last meeting, I thought I would give him the honor of reading his poem first. She handed him the poem.

Matthew flushed a bit. He cleared his throat, and started reading.

When he finished, he looked up at Moira, who was looking back at him. Then he heard a kind of whimper coming from down the table, as did everyone else. He saw a young woman put her hands to her face and then she burst out sobbing. Matthew was momentarily stunned. For a minute, no one spoke. Some just stared at her with sympathetic looks, others stared down at the table. The woman next to her put her hand on the girl's back.

Finally, Moira, in a soft voice, said, "Megan, can you tell us why that upset you?"

Megan shook her head, her elbows on the table, her hands still covering her face. Then she said, in a choked voice, "My Dad killed himself. When I was fourteen." She started sobbing again, then abruptly got up from the table and left the room. One of the other women started to get up to go after her, but Moira said, "No. Don't. Leave her alone for now. I think she needs to be alone for a bit." The woman sat down. There were some long moments of silence. Finally Moira spoke up, in a gentle voice. "Words, and writing, can be a very powerful thing, as you just saw. And as we just heard from Matthew's poem. Would anyone like to comment on his poem?"

The woman who'd put her hand on Megan's back, said, "I thought it was very sad. I almost cried too. It was very moving."

A few people nodded in agreement.

During the rest of the hour, they went around the table and shared their poems and comments. Matthew, to his shame, was only half listening to the others, because his mind kept wandering to Moira, even when he wasn't looking at her. One time she caught him staring at her, and he was sure she'd held his gaze a bit too long for it to be a normal look. Something in him stirred.

On his way back to his room afterward, Moira's gaze filled his thoughts and imagination. In a matter of days, if not hours, Matthew had developed a crush on. She was older, probably around forty, but he found her very sexy, and he was attracted to her outgoing and unconventional personality.

The next day he saw her at the nurses' station, and walked up to the counter. She looked up at him. "Hey, Matthew, how are you?"

"Hi, Moira. I'm doing okay today."

"That's wonderful," she said. "Do you need some help with something?"

"Well . . . umm, I have level two privileges, and I was wondering if you'd be willing to take me out for a walk, since it's time now for level twos to go out with an escort, if they can find one."

She nodded. "Sure, Matthew. I'd be glad to. Just give me about five minutes."

He felt a little thrill pass through him. "Great. Thank you, Moira. I really appreciate it."

He waited a few minutes while she finished a few things, and signed himself out on the chalkboard.

Then she came around the counter. "Are you ready?" she asked.

"Desperately," he replied. He was very excited.

"Okay. You signed yourself out?"

"Yes."

"Alright. Let's go for a walk." She led him down the hallway to the door, and unlocked it. He was so happy to get away from the unit, and doubly pleased because he was with Moira. They rode the elevator down, and exited the hospital. They started walking down a path towards a scenic vista on the grounds of the hospital. Neither of them spoke.

Finally, Matthew stopped. "Moira," he said. She stopped and looked at him. He looked her in the eyes. "Moira, I don't know how else to say this, so I'll just say it. I'm very attracted to you. I think you're a dynamite woman, and I was wondering if, when I get out of here, if I could take you out to dinner."

She visibly stiffened. A look of consternation came over her, but Matthew also detected a flash of mutual attraction.

"Matthew," she said. "You're an attractive guy. You're handsome, creative and smart. You're also wearing a wedding band. If circumstances were different, I'd love to go out with you, and I'm very flattered that you've asked. But I'm a nurse here, and I have professional and ethical obligations . . ."

"I know," he interrupted. "But I'm talking about once I'm out of here. I mean, once I'm out of here, you're not my nurse anymore, and I'm not your patient, right? And I'm in the midst of a divorce."

"Yes, but Matthew, you're in a hospital. And I sincerely hope that you never have to come back here again. But what if you do? How can I be a professional, a nurse to you as my patient, at the same time that I'm fucking you?"

Matthew flushed at her bluntness. He didn't say anything, but he understood. He just looked at her.

"Matthew, I'm very flattered by the invitation. But it can't happen. You understand that, right?"

He nodded. "Yes."

A look of warmth came over her. "Hey. I understand loneliness. Believe me. But some woman out there is going to find you, and snatch you up. You're a hot ticket, believe me."

"No, I'm damaged goods," he said. "I'm in the loony bin."

"That's because you're ill, Matthew. It's no different from being hospitalized for any other disease. If a girl is too dumb to understand that, then she doesn't deserve you anyway."

He looked at her for a long moment. "Thank you," he said. "You're a nice person, Moira. I guess that's why I'm attracted to you." He smiled. "Not to mention that you're incredibly sexy."

She smiled back and punched him lightly in the chest. "Cut it out. You're very bad, you know that? What am I going to do with you?"

He smiled again. "Whatever your heart desires."

"All right," she smiled." That's enough out of you. It's time to go back," and she started walking.

"Aw, come on," he said, following her.

"Shut your mouth. Not another word or I'm going to revoke your privileges."

"Yes, Nurse Diesel."

"Don't push me! I mean it!" she said, looking back and obviously suppressing a smile.

"Okay, okay. I'll be good." And then, without thinking, he reached forward and pinched her ass.

She started, then quickly turned around. She looked angry. "Listen! I'm serious! Cut the shit, okay? My job is at stake here."

Matthew realized he'd crossed the line, and regretted it. "I'm sorry, Moira. I'm very sorry. I shouldn't have done that. I'm very sorry. Please forgive me."

Her look softened. "It's okay. But enough, okay? I meant what I said."

He nodded, his eyes to the ground. "I understand. It won't happen again."

"Okay," she said. She turned and continued walking, with Matthew a few steps behind. He felt like a scolded dog.

Chapter Four

Matthew was discharged a few days later from the locked unit into an outpatient program which consisted mostly of support groups. He could go home to his apartment at the end of the day. He was pleased to have been released from the unit, and yet he felt the familiar darkness of depression descending upon him very quickly. His first night home he took out a razor blade and cut up his left wrist. He felt relieved as he watched the bright red blood splash all over the white porcelain sink. He had previously purchased some gauze for just such occasions, so he ran some cold water over his wrist, which was still bleeding, and then tightly wrapped the gauze around his wrist and taped it.

The following day, after a night of drinking and dozing off and on in his chair till afternoon, he missed all his out-patient groups. He decided to go out. Despite his continuing depression and self-destructive urges, or perhaps because of all this, he decided he would revel in his misery and self-disgust by going to a strip club. He still had some sex drive left, and a partial outlet—sex for the eyes—might slake his thirst. And if it lifted his spirits even the slightest bit, it would be worth it. He hadn't been to a strip club since his brother-in-law's bachelor party six or seven years ago. He walked unsteadily to his car and drove to a club a few towns over. It was only early afternoon, and as his eyes adjusted to the dim interior he saw the place was nearly empty of customers. He ordered a beer and took a seat next to the stage runway. An attractive brunette was on, and he watched as she swung around a pole, clad only in garters and stockings. He placed some dollar bills on the edge of the raised floor and watched with a mixture of lust, embarrassment and shame as the girl laid down before him and spread her legs, revealing the soft butterfly of her sex. This sight, coupled with the throbbing music, aroused him. When she finished her set, she came out of a side room and sat down next to him.

She smiled at him. "What's a cute, respectable looking guy like you doing in a place like this?"

He blushed. "Well, I might ask you the same thing."

She laughed. "First of all, I'm not a cute, respectable looking guy. And second, I work here. A girl's got to make a living, you know."

"Point taken."

"Would you be willing to buy a hard-working girl a drink?

"Sure, What would you like?"

"A bourbon on ice."

He went to the bar and ordered two of the same. Several strippers and rough-looking customers were sitting at the bar, drinking and chatting in low voices. He went back to the girl and handed her the drink.

"I'm Michelle," she said.

"I'm Matthew," he replied. "So, tell me, is that your real name?"

"Yes, it is," she said. "And I don't give it out very often."

"So, what made you give it to me?"

"Your eyes."

"My eyes?" He was genuinely surprised.

"Yes, your eyes. I can tell by the eyes whether a customer is a sleaze, or just a lonely guy. Or both. And in many cases," she said, pointing to his wedding band, "a lonely, married guy. You strike me as a lonely, married gentleman."

He nodded. "Yup. That's me. A lonely, married gentleman. Though I'm not really much of a gentleman when you get right down to it."

"Oh, the mysterious type, eh? Well, you're incredibly cute, and with eyes like those you could go a long way."

"A long way? What do you mean?"

"Let me give you a hint."

She stood up, took his hand, and led him into a dark corner of the club. She motioned for him to sit on the corner sofa. "Have you ever had a lap dance?"

His face felt hot. He shook his head. "No."

She smiled down at him. "Okay, sweetie, you're about to get one. You just sit there. You don't have to do a thing, except slip me a twenty when I'm done."

He was nervous. "Okay. I can do that."

She knelt on the sofa, straddling him, her hands in his hair. She began gyrating her hips, grinding into him, and he felt a surge in his groin. Her breasts were inches from his face. He cupped his hands on the sides of her breasts, but she pulled his hands down. "Sorry, sweetie. You can't do that. House rules. I can fondle you, but you can't fondle me. That bouncer over there is very protective, if you know what I mean."

"I'm sorry."

"Hey, no problem." She lifted his chin and looked into his eyes. "Besides, there are ways to get around it, if you really want to."

"What do you mean?"

She shook her head. "Oh, for chrissake, Matthew, do I have to spell it out for you?"

The light went on in his head. "Oh," he said.

She leaned in and spoke softly into his ear. "I'm very, very good."

"I'll bet you are."

She sat back a bit, and smiled. Again, she spoke softly, just above a whisper. "Are you willing to put your money where your mouth is?"

He didn't even hesitate. "Yes," he said.

She smiled, then slid off his legs and knelt on the floor between his knees. She ran her hands up and down his thighs, then messaged the bulge in his pants. She pressed her mouth against it. "Mmm. I bet you taste delicious," she said, and coyly smiled up at him.

His throat constricted, and he cleared his throat. "How does this work?" he asked.

"I get off work at six," she said. "Just meet me in the parking lot a few minutes after six."

"I'd like that. I'd like that very much." He cleared his throat again. "Umm, how much should I bring?"

"Three hundred,"

"Would you come to my apartment? It's about fifteen minutes away."

"Sure. If you want, you can have me the whole night. Would you like that, Mr. Matthew?"

"Yes, I'd love to have you all night."

"That would be four hundred and fifty, then."

"That's fine."

She continued her lap dance for several more minutes. When she stopped, she kissed him on the lips, then stood up and smiled at him. He gave her thirty dollars.

"Thank you. Six o'clock?" she asked.

He nodded. "Six o'clock. Umm, is there anything you'd like to drink when you come to my place?"

"Hmm. How about some champagne? Great sex calls for a celebration, don't you think?"

"Yeah, especially for me."

You poor man." She shook her head. "Well, we're gonna take care of that tonight, Sweetie. I think two bottles of champagne are in order, because you're gonna get laid, Sweetie, fucked till you drop, and that deserves a real celebration." She bent down and kissed him again, running her fingers through his hair. "God, you're cute. I'm gonna enjoy this." She turned and walked away, heading for the door beside the stage. She turned, looked back at him and gave a little wave. He smiled.

He went back to his seat by the stage, and drank for a while as several other dancers went through their routines. A few more customers came into the club, probably just off of work, and sat by the stage with their drinks. After a while, not seeing Michelle on stage again, he left and headed back to his room, stopping on the way to buy a couple bottles of champagne, some ice, and a bottle of bourbon. When he got to his room, he put the champagne on ice, poured himself a bourbon and paced around his room, waiting for six o'clock to come. It seemed an eternity.

Finally, just before six, he drove back to the club. He got out of his car, and leaned against it, smoking a cigarette. He felt nervous and guilty, and had a brief urge to get back in his car and drive away. But he didn't. He wanted this.

A few minutes past six Michelle came out of the club. She was wearing a short, skin-tight black dress and very high heels. He flushed with excitement.

"Hey, gorgeous," she said.

"Hey, gorgeous," he replied. They smiled at each other.

"Oooh, a Jaguar," she said. "Very, very nice. You know how to impress a girl."

"Thank you. She's one of my passions."

"She?" she said with a laugh. "Well, I don't blame you. She's almost as gorgeous as you. But I'll bet she's never fucked you."

He laughed. "No, she's rebuffed all my advances. So, may I give you a ride, Miss?"

"Yes. Do that. You give me a ride now, and I'll give you a ride later. How's that?"

He smiled. "That's a deal."

He opened the door for her. Her dress was so short he could see the tops of her thighs as she got in. She looked up and saw him staring at her legs. She gave him a devilish look. "You naughty boy. Must you be so brazen in your lust?"

"I'm sorry. It's just that your legs are so beautiful."

"Just my legs? You really know how to hurt a girl." She laughed. "You know, you're just a rude, lecherous sleaze. I thought you were a gentleman."

He smiled. "Looks are deceiving." He enjoyed the flirtatious banter.

"Hurry up," she said. "I'm getting horny."

"Yes, ma'am." He closed the door and walked around the car. The guilt had been swept away. He felt great. He put the car in gear and headed for his apartment.

"Did you get the champagne?" she asked.

"I certainly did. And a bottle of bourbon, too."

"Oh, you're a party animal, huh?"

He glanced at her and grinned. "I aim to please."

"So do I," she said, and she kissed him on the cheek.

He popped a Coldplay CD into the player.

"Oh, cool," she said. "I love Coldplay. You have very good taste."

"Yeah, they're my favorite band."

A few minutes later he turned into the parking lot and found a spot. He went around the car and opened the door for her. "I'm sorry, but it's not a very fancy place."

"All we need is a bed, Sweetie."

"Well, it does have that, so I guess it's okay."

He led her upstairs and unlocked the door to his apartment. He was ashamed of it. "Here we are. Classy, huh?"

She wrapped her arms around his waist and kissed him deeply. He was thrilled. His whole body was electric. He marveled that she had this power over him.

"You're trembling," she said. "Don't be nervous, Sweetie. I don't bite. Unless of course you want me too," and she winked.

"I'm just excited," he said. They kissed again. "Would you like some champagne?"

"I thought you'd never ask."

He uncorked a bottle, and poured the champagne into the plastic champagne glasses he'd bought at the liquor store. "I even got us some champagne glasses. Aren't you impressed?"

"Yes. Nice touch," she said. "Maybe you're a gentleman after all."

They raised their plastic glasses, touched them together, and drank.

"Um, let me get this out of the way," he said, feeling awkward, and he handed her the money.

"Thank you, darling," she said. "I like customers who pay their bills on time. They get extra points in bed." She tucked the money into her purse.

"Well," he said.

She sat down on the bed, grabbed a pillow, and put it behind her back, leaning against the headboard. She patted the bed next to her. "You. Come here."

He sat down next to her.

"Do you like porn movies?" she asked.

Matthew was just then sipping his champagne, and almost spit it out. "Porn?"

"Yeah, porn," she said. "You know, movies with men and women fucking. You've heard of them, right?"

"Well, yes. As a matter of fact, I watched one last night."

"Oh, you bad boy. Did you jerk off?"

He blushed. "Umm, yes. I did."

"Well, that's good. It fits the picture. Lonely gentleman who doesn't get any pussy, watching porn and getting off by himself."

"Yeah. I guess that's true."

"Hey, nothing to be ashamed of. I watch porn all the time and make myself come."

"You do?"

"Hell yes. What's better than a good orgasm before going to sleep?"

"Good point."

"Well, just by sheer coincidence," she said, "I happen to have a fine motion picture in my purse." She took her purse off the side table and pulled out a DVD. "Here. This'll get your juices flowing." She handed him the DVD.

"I don't know if I can handle watching a porn movie with a girl like you sitting next to me."

She smiled. "You can't watch a movie with an innocent girl-next-door like me?"

He laughed. "Something tells me you are not all that innocent."

"Shame on you," she said. "Whatever gave you that impression?"

"Oh, I don't know. Just a hunch, I guess."

"Just a hunch, huh? You're being quite forward, you know."

"I know. I apologize, Miss."

"So, Mr. Matthew, are you going to put that movie on? And I need some more champagne, if you please. You're not a very good host, you know."

He laughed, and reached for the bottle. "Please accept my apologies."

"I'll think about it."

He went over to the disc player and put on the movie. "Here we are," he said. "A nice, family Disney film. A sequel to 'Mary Poppins' I think."

She laughed. "Yeah, well, you'll see Mary getting fucked from the very start. I can't stand those porn flicks that try to pretend they're real movies and have these ridiculous scenes with horrible actors. Just cut to the chase and give me the sex."

"You're quite forward, Miss."

"Oh, yes, I am. What's better than sex, Mr. Matthew? Is there a better, healthier activity in life?"

"Hmm. I'll have to think about that."

"No, you don't."

He laughed. "No, I don't."

"Speaking of health," she said. "You'll need to wear these, my love," and she produced a condom from her purse on the nightstand. "Can't take any chances. Even with a virgin like you."

He laughed again. "Absolutely, my dear. But I assure you I am clean as a whistle."

"I'll bet I can make you come just slipping it onto you. And I hope to put many of them on you."

"Mmm. You really know how to tease a guy."

"Hush," she said. "There's a very fine film playing here."

"Yes. There is."

They watched for few minutes.

"Michelle. Why do you do this?"

"Oh, please. Don't get all moral and philosophical on me."

"I'm sorry."

"I'm the only one who gets to be philosophical here." She gulped her champagne. "So, hey, it's nothing to me if you don't want to talk about it, and it's none of my business anyway, but I can't help wondering. What exactly are you doing here? I mean, despite your apparent lack of a sex life, doesn't your wife kind of notice if you're not in bed with her? I mean, you do have that gold thing on your finger."

He refilled his plastic glass, drank half of it, and was silent for a long moment. "I got caught red-handed not having sex with our nanny."

"You have a nanny?"

"Yeah."

"Okay, and let me get this straight. You got nailed for not having sex with your nanny? Like, if you'd fucked her everything would have been cool with the wife? This seems a little bass-ackward, my friend. Some sort of explanation is in order here."

"Well, Jenna and I—that's our nanny—we were having a drink and wound up doing a little necking, and my wife, who was supposed to be out of town, walked in on us. The thing is, I had already called a halt with Jenna, told her I couldn't do it because I was married and all, and then my wife walked in."

"So you got busted for sorta-kinda making out with the nanny."

"Yeah, I guess. But my wife, quite reasonably, thought we'd been fucking, especially since Jenna's panties were on the floor."

"Her panties! You were a doing a little more than necking, my friend." She shook her head. "So tell me about this nanny. Is she hot?"

"Yeah, she is. She was the runner up in the Miss Iowa beauty contest."

"Oh my god. You hired a beauty queen for your nanny? What the fuck was your wife smoking? That was a recipe for disaster. I mean, men are men. Your wife hires a frickin' Playboy bunny to live with you? What the hell did she expect? Are you serious?"

"Yes. I'm dead serious."

"Jesus Christ. I would have hired an eighty year old lady with warts who'd forgotten what a cock was. How old is this nanny?"

"Twenty-two."

"Okay, just a dumb kid looking for a thrill and testing her powers over her handsome boss. I don't blame her. Your wife is the one who needs her head examined. What was she thinking?"

"Michelle, I get where you're coming from, but my wife trusted me implicitly. I don't think she ever considered the possibility—I mean, we're married, and I'd never done anything, even remotely, to break that trust."

"Okay, I understand that," she said. "But you don't leave candy lying around children without expecting them to eat it, right?"

"I know. But she trusted me. It was my own fault. Not hers."

"Jesus Christ," she said, shaking her head. "And when did all this go down?"

"A few months ago."

"Man. It didn't take you long to bounce back."

"Well, I hadn't planned on this happening . . . meeting you."

"Well, it's a damn fortunate thing for you that you did, Buster. You need this."

"I do need this," he said. "I haven't had sex in almost two years."

Michelle almost spit out her champagne. Her mouth fell open. "Two years! Jesus Christ, I would have tried to fuck the nanny, too! Oh, you poor man you. I'm going to have to really give it to you tonight to work out all that pent up frustration."

"I guess that's why I'm here."

"Well, I guess so, Sweetie. No wonder."

He took her hand, sipped some champagne, and gave his attention to the movie. A muscle-bound guy had a girl up on a countertop, her legs open wide, and was pumping her hard. After a few minutes, he pulled out, groaned, and shot his semen all over her breasts and stomach while she gasped and groaned as realistically as she could.

"This is Academy Award stuff," Michelle said. "But it's making me hot. You, too, I can see. I'll bet you'd like to shoot your jiz all over me, Mr. Gentleman. Am I right?"

He turned on his side and began kissing and fondling her breasts through her skin-tight dress. "I refuse to answer that on the grounds that it may incriminate me." He was very aroused now. As he ran his hand over her body, his breathing became shorter. She placed her hand on his crotch.

"Somebody's getting very, very excited," she said. She kissed him, thrusting her tongue into his mouth. Then she pulled back and gave him a coy smile. "You do know what men and women do, right? What they do to each other?"

"Geez, I'm not a virgin, you know."

"Good, good," she said. "And you know how to please a woman, right? You're not one of these wham bam minutemen, are you? I expect a gentleman like you to be well versed in the art of lovemaking, Mr. Matthew. I don't want to spend the whole night sleeping, you know. That would be a shameful waste of your money."

"No. I want my money's worth."

"Good. Pour me some more champagne, and take your pants off. And take my panties off while you're at it."

Matthew was nearly breathless with excitement. His encounter with Jenna had awakened and enflamed a tremendous, pent-up desire to make love to a woman, and it had been burning inside him ever since. He marveled at the fact that he was about to get laid by a beautiful young woman. The guilt he'd felt earlier had been washed away by sheer desire.

They embraced and groped each other, quickly shedding their clothes. Then she stopped, and he saw her staring at his bandaged wrist. He tensed up. There was a long pause. "I wasn't trying to kill myself."

She looked at him with a look of wonder and concern. "Then what exactly were you trying to do?"

"I was punishing myself. I've been depressed, and I was just inflicting pain on myself. They're superficial wounds. I wasn't trying to kill myself." He paused. "It's kind of hard to explain."

She looked at his wrist again. Then she lifted his wrist to her lips and kissed the bandage.

Matthew almost felt like crying. Neither of them said anything. Then she leaned in and kissed him deeply, pushing her tongue into his mouth.

He felt himself suddenly letting go. He felt free, and with her encouragement he took her every way he'd ever fantasized about. To his surprise, he was able to keep at it for hours, having several orgasms along the way, and was pleased that he was able to make her come repeatedly as well. He had no doubts that she was getting off for real.

Finally, at some point in the night, having had another tremendous orgasm, he laid back, his heart pounding and his breath short. "Oh, my god," he said. "This has been incredible, Michelle. I'm totally spent."

"You're such a light-weight," she said, even as she was still breathless herself. They were silent for a moment. Then she said, "You're pretty amazing. I mean that. I'm not trying to give you a customer line. You really are an amazing lover. I almost feel guilty taking your money for so much great sex."

"Thanks," he said. "A rebate would be welcome." It was all the energy he had left to speak.

"Don't get cocky," she said, softly. She turned on her side, toward him, her head and hand resting on his chest, and they both soon fell asleep.

When he awoke, at dawn, Michelle was gone. She'd left a note on the pillow: *Thanks for a fantastic night. You are a great lover. I almost feel guilty taking your* money, I enjoyed it so much. But a girl's got to make a living, right? You know where I work. Come see me any time you need some TLC, or just to get laid. Michelle." There was a lipstick kiss at the bottom.

For a minute Matthew felt happy and sad at the same time. His night had been a fantasy come true. But the larger picture upset him. He'd just spent the night with a hooker. A nice one, a perfect one no doubt, but a hooker all the same. As he laid there in bed depression crashed over him like a huge wave. Again the thoughts of razors, pills, guns, and jumps. He was lost and out of control.

Later that day he has driving to a bookstore when he noticed that a favorite song of his on the radio was playing too slow. He had heard this song a hundred times, and knew that there was no mistaking it: the song was playing too slow. But he simply chalked it up to a problem with the radio station's disc player, and switched to another station. But then he noticed the same thing with another familiar song. It was playing too slow. A surge of fear passed through him. He turned to another station, to another familiar song, and again, it was playing too slow—even slower than the previous songs; the voices were barely singing. Matthew became frightened and alarmed. He turned off the radio. He tried to forget about it, but the memory of the moving plant and the coffee maker crowded in, and once again feared that he was going insane. Again, the desire for death washed over him.

At the bookstore he purchased a book by Sartre, *Being and Nothingness*, and another by Martin Heidegger, *Being and Time*. Both were massive existentialist tomes, and he hoped that they might speak to him and maybe even explain the world to him. He was not disappointed. Both of them were dense and difficult reading, but he grasped hold of them as a drowning man grasps a life preserver. The world they depicted was the world that he himself was living in. Misery loves company, and he'd found a philosophical school in existentialism that provided him that company. In those books he found a sort of negative salvation; a philosophy that justified his self-hatred, his loneliness, his despair about the world around him and the actions of his fellow human beings.

It was a marvelously bleak philosophy: no god; no souls; no destiny; no human nature; no afterlife. There was only the vertigo and angst about our being the authors of our own lives, that everything we do is our choice, and that we are the sum of our choices. We live in a state of perpetual self-delusion and hide from the responsibility for our lives, and of being authentic. Even consciousness is reduced to a sort of nothingness, which, nonetheless, defines us, just as the holes, the empty spaces, in Swiss cheese define Swiss cheese. Matthew thought of himself as a hole, an empty space in the shell of a human body.

Around this time, for bizarre reasons Matthew couldn't fathom, he gradually acquired via mail order, over a period of weeks, reproductions of all the elements of a German SS officer's uniform. One evening, on impulse, he put it on. He stood before the mirror as he placed on the peaked visor cap with the skull and cross-bones emblem, and admired the infamous black uniform. He was adjusting the swastika arm band when he heard a muffled crash from the apartment below, and then a woman's scream. He went into the room and dropped to the floor, ear to the rug, and heard her struggling to cry out again, but someone was obviously covering her mouth. He heard a muffled cry for help. At that he raced out of the apartment, down the stairs, and banged at the apartment door.

"What's going on!" he yelled in his sternest voice. "Do you need help?"

"Yes, I do! I do!" the woman screamed.

"She's fine!" the man repeated.

"Get out!" she yelled.

"I think you better come out, buddy, or I'm calling the police."

"Fine!" the man barked. "Gladly, you fucking cunt!" The door suddenly opened and a short man in his twenties with a crew cut and tattooed arms came out. Matthew stepped back, and as the man headed quickly to the stairs he looked back in surprise at Matthew in his Nazi uniform and said, "What the fuck?" But he didn't stop, and ran down the stairway to the first floor and out the door.

Matthew looked back into the apartment and saw the woman, a blonde in her thirties, sitting on the floor in the middle of the room. Her lower lip was split and bleeding, and she was crying. She was staring at Matthew through her tears.

"Are you okay?" he asked. "Do you want me to call the police?"

"I don't know," she said. "I'm scared. Would you do it for me?"

"Yes. Sure," he said. "My apartment is right upstairs. Why don't you come up with me, and I'll make the call."

He led her upstairs and into his apartment. He motioned for her to sit in his easy chair. She was staring at him in wonder. Then she noticed his cigarettes on the end table. "Can I have one of your cigarettes?" she asked.

"Sure." He went over and lit it for her. Then he pulled out his cell phone and dialed 911. When the operator answered, he briefly explained the situation, and told her his name and address. He noticed that the blonde woman was staring at him again. The operator told him that the police would be there shortly. "Thank you," he said, and hung up. He looked at the woman. "They'll be right over," he said. He was feeling more and more embarrassed by the moment, standing there in his Nazi uniform.

"Thank you," she said. "Thank you for helping me."

"Hey, no problem."

There was an awkward silence.

"Why are you dressed up like a Nazi?" she finally asked.

Matthew blushed. He didn't know what to say. He took off his visor cap, and turned away. "Would you like a drink?" he asked. "I could sure use one." He realized that the whole incident downstairs had left him trembling.

"Yeah. I could use one, too," she said. "Thank you."

He poured two bourbons and gave one to her. It was apparent that she'd already had a few drinks. He gulped his drink, and was about to go into the bathroom to take off his uniform, when the doorbell rang. "Damn," he said.

He left the apartment, went down to the building entrance and saw two cops at the door, with a squad car parked behind them. He saw the looks on their faces as they saw his uniform. He felt like a complete idiot. Why is this happening to me, he wondered. He opened the door.

"Are you Mr. St. Clare?" one of them asked.

"Yes. I'm the one who called."

"Where is the victim?"

"She's upstairs in my apartment. I brought her up there to wait till you came." He turned and headed up the stairs. He was very conscious of his jackboots as they climbed the stairs, knowing that his boots would be just above them on the stairs.

When they entered the apartment, he was relieved that the officers focused their attention on the woman, and not him. He stood in the kitchenette, off to the side, while they questioned her and took pictures of her bruised face. Then one of the officers came over to him and asked him what he'd seen, and would he be able to identify the man who'd beaten her. Matthew nodded. The policeman asked him for his phone number. "You may be called as a witness if charges are made."

Matthew nodded again. "That's fine."

There was an awkward pause. "So tell me," the officer asked at last. "Why are you dressed in a Nazi uniform?"

Matthew had an answer this time. "I'm an actor," he lied. "It's for a play I'm doing."

"A play," the officer said, clearly not believing him. "What play would that be, if you don't mind my asking?"

"Umm, it's a Jean-Paul Sartre play, *The Condemned of Altona*. It's about a Nazi war criminal.

"Oh," the officer said, registering some surprise.

Matthew got the feeling that he'd actually convinced the officer, or at least half-convinced him, anyway.

The officer turned to his partner and said, "Let's bring her down to her apartment. We can finish talking to her there, and let this man have his apartment back."

As they filed out the door, the woman stopped and asked Matthew his name.

"Well, thank you, Matthew, for helping me."

"No problem. I'm just glad you're okay."

"For a Nazi, you're pretty cute."

Matthew flushed. Then they were gone. He closed the door and went into the bathroom. He looked at himself in the mirror. A breeze of sanity blew through, and he was horrified. "But," he said aloud, "You did a good thing. You helped that woman. So what if you're wearing an SS uniform. You didn't do anything wrong."

He continued to stare at himself for a few moments. Then he ripped open his tunic, buttons popping and falling to the floor. He took it off as fast as he could and threw it into the bathtub. He wanted it to go away. He thought about burning it, but realized it would set off the smoke alarm. He went to his easy chair, sat down and pulled off his jack-boots. He went into the kitchenette and dropped them into the trash can. He felt dirty and ashamed. He poured himself another drink and dropped down into his easy chair to unwind. As he was unwinding, he pondered the question of why he had donned an SS uniform. Maybe, he thought, it was because he hated himself. Hating yourself is pretty easy when you're wearing an SS uniform.

He realized he was going off the deep end. He realized he was sick. He went into the bathroom and began cutting his wrist with a razor. Once again, with blood streaming down his arm, he traced a swastika on his cheek, then painted a cross on his other cheek. Good and evil. It felt good. He was a confused wreck.

While smearing the blood on his face, he noticed the reflection of his wedding band in the mirror, and suddenly felt sick. He needed to take it off, not because he wanted to forget his marriage, but because the sight of it reminded him of the trust he had broken, the vows he had smashed, which had destroyed his marriage. He tried to take it off, but his finger had thickened over the years, and no matter how hard he pulled, he couldn't get it over his knuckle. As his wrist continued to bleed, he rubbed some blood over the knuckle and ring, and with some pain to his finger, finally managed to pull off the ring. He burst into tears.

After a while he pulled himself together a bit, washed his face and wrapped up his wrist. He picked up his wedding ring and wondered what to do with it. He looked around the room for a place to put it, then remembered the sweater vest. He pulled open a dresser drawer, and at the bottom of the drawer, found the wool vest he'd worn the night he'd proposed to Helen. In the pocket of the vest was the cork from the bottle of wine they'd shared that night. He'd kept it in that vest pocket all the years of his marriage. The sight of the vest, and the cork, brought back the tears. He placed the ring into the pocket with the cork, carefully folded the vest and placed it back in the drawer. He felt like Judas. And Judas had hanged himself. He decided to go to bed in order to escape the heartache and dangerous thoughts. He cried himself to sleep.

A week or so later, back in the outpatient program and miserably depressed, he stopped on the way to the hospital and bought a bottle of sleeping pills and a bottle of scotch. He went to the first group that day, but afterwards he retrieved the pills and booze from his car and walked to a spot near the McLean administration building, overlooking the large bowl of grass, trees and handsome old buildings below. There were some Adirondack chairs there, and he sat down in the one that had the best view. He had brought his camera with him, and as he washed down handfuls of pills with whisky, he took pictures of his surroundings, to leave a photographic record of his last moments of life. He finished the bottle of eighty pills, and about half of the whisky. He sat back in the chair and waited to die. But after a few minutes, as he grew groggy, and without any thought, he stood up and walked to the building where his psychiatrist had his office. Dr. Mendel was practically the only person Matthew thought could help him. And he knew he needed help, very quickly.

He entered the building and went downstairs to Dr. Mendel's office. His door was closed, but Matthew knocked on it anyway. A moment later, Dr. Mendel opened the door slightly, and said, "Matthew. I'm with a patient right now. Can it wait?"

"Doctor, I've just taken eighty sleeping pills and a lot of booze. I think I need help."

Dr. Mendel's expression changed, and he opened the door wide, turning at the same time to the girl sitting in his office. "Brenda. Excuse me. This is an emergency."

Matthew heard the girl say, "Go, doctor. I'll call you."

Dr. Mendel calmly escorted Matthew from the building.

"Where are we going, Doctor?"

"We're going to the admissions building."

Matthew was beginning to feel blurry and weak. He felt Dr. Mendel's arm around his waist. They made it to the admissions building, and Dr. Mendel helped Matthew to a sofa. The doctor said a few words to the woman at the desk, then came over to Matthew. The last thing Matthew saw was Dr. Mendel's face leaning close, telling him to hold on, that help was on the way. Then he passed out.

When he awoke he was in a room at Mount Auburn Hospital. They had already pumped his stomach, and were now trying to get him to drink a bottle of liquid charcoal. He feebly sipped it, and decided it was the most horrible thing he'd ever tasted in his life. But the nurse made him drink it all, explaining that it was absorbing whatever pills were still in his stomach.

The following day he was taken by ambulance back to McLean.

Chapter Five

Back on the unit, one of the first people he saw was Moira. He lowered his eyes in shame. Shame because he was back on the unit, and shame because he'd propositioned her the last time. But she came up to him and said, without a hint of anything but compassion, "Hi, Matthew. I'm sorry that you've had to come back here, and that you're having such a difficult time."

Matthew just looked at her a moment, then said, "Thank you, Moira."

"I hope, when you're feeling a little better, that you decide to rejoin my writing group."

He nodded slightly, but didn't say anything.

"I'll be around if you ever need to talk."

"Thank you."

She walked back to the nurses' station.

One of the patients, an older woman who'd been here in his first go round, came up to him and gave him a friendly hug. "I'm sorry you had to come back, Matthew."

"Thank you, Fran," he replied. "How are you doing? I thought you were being released?"

"Well, I had a sort of breakdown ... I seem to take one step forward and two steps back. But I'm having ECT treatments, and maybe they'll soon help me."

"Well, I'm sorry you've been struggling, but pleased to hear that you're still hopeful."

"Thanks," she said. "Well, I've got a group to attend. I'll see you around."

Matthew walked back to his new room and sat on the bed. There was no roommate. He couldn't believe he was here again, and so soon.

The following day Matthew declined to go to any groups. In fact, he never got out of bed, except when he went to the kitchen once to get some graham crackers and juice. The staff tended to give new patients, even ones who'd recently been discharged and come back, a bit of slack for the first day or so, so he knew he wouldn't be bothered. For now, he had the room to himself. That's another thing that new arrivals generally get, just to let them have a bit of privacy while they decompress and acclimate to the unit. Matthew slept through most of that day.

The next morning he felt a little better, or at least enough to get out of bed. He went to the morning community meeting, and had some breakfast. He felt he had graduated up to a quasi-functional state. He went to a few of the groups, though he said nothing. He just sat there listening to the other patients. However, after dinner that night, as he sat reading in the common room, one of the patients, a dark-haired, attractive woman about his own age, sat at a nearby table, writing in a notebook or journal. He noticed that she had a silver pentacle around her neck. This sparked his curiosity, so he went to her table and asked if he could join her.

"Sure," she said, then resumed her writing.

"I noticed your pentacle," he said, a bit shyly. "Are you a witch?"

She looked up at him. "I prefer the term 'Wiccan.' But in common parlance, yes, I am a witch."

"That's cool," he said.

A cynical look came over her. "Cool?"

"Well, I mean . . . well, I've never met a witch before."

"Well, you've met one now. Careful what you say, because I might turn you into a rodent."

Matthew was about to laugh at the joke, but then he saw that her expression hadn't changed a bit. "Do you really believe you can do that?"

"Of course not. I was just trying to play to your probable ignorance about wiccans."

"Oh." Matthew felt awkward. "Umm . . . Despite what you might think, I have a lot of respect for wiccans."

"How nice," she said.

"No, really. I've actually done some reading on the subject."

"And?"

"Well, like I said, I have lot of respect for wiccans."

"And why is that?"

"I don't know . . . I guess it's because of your independence, your rejection of the mainstream religions."

"Okay," she said. "That's a fair response. So tell me, what is your understanding of wicca?"

She was putting Matthew on the spot. He thought for a moment. "Well, to me wicca is about a connection, a spiritual connection, with the natural world, with the Earth, the sun, the moon, and with other people. And you believe that you have natural powers to make a positive difference on people and events."

Her expression softened a bit. "Not bad," she said. "Not bad."

Matthew was pleased. "See? I'm not as ignorant as I look. I really do understand that as a witch you don't run around with pointy black hats, flying around on broomsticks and casting evil spells. You don't even have warts on your face."

She smiled. "Well, that puts you ahead of most other people, especially fundamentalist Christians who think we should all be burned at the stake and sent straight to Hell. 'Thou shalt not suffer a witch to live,' as the Bible says."

"Well, I'm not a Christian," he said.

"What are you?"

"An atheist. I used to be a Christian, but then the scales fell from my eyes, and that was that."

"I used to be a Christian myself," she said.

"How did you go from being a Christian to being a witch?"

"I read the Bible."

"I don't understand."

"Have you read the Bible?"

"Parts of it." He paused. "Well, a little of it."

"That's always amazed me, that so few Christians have actually read the Bible, except for the occasional snippet from the gospels, or a psalm here or there. I'm not attacking you, because you're no longer a Christian. But I don't understand how Christians can read all these junky novels and gooey self-help books, without reading the one book central to their religion. But then again, if they actually read it, they might quit their church."

"Well, you said you used to be a Christian. Did you read it?

"Every word."

"But what is it about the Bible that repulsed you so much?"

"It was mostly the Old Testament that pissed me off. I mean, most of it is pure, hateful garbage. You've got this ogre of a god either killing people left and right, or directing others to kill left and right. Read the book of Joshua. It's nothing less than genocide, commanded by God. God's chosen people didn't stop at killing adults and babies; they went on to kill all their animals, too. I mean, the whole O.T. is full of genocide, rape, murder, incest, ethnocentrism, fairy tales, testosterone, contradiction—you name it. The word of God? Wow. Some God."

Matthew detected some anger behind her words. "Well, what about the New Testament?" he asked.

"Actually," she replied, "I don't have a problem with the New Testament itself, but rather the Christians, particularly the liberal churches, who pick and choose what they want to believe and what they simply ignore because it offends their sensibilities."

"Such as?"

"Such as Hell. Show me a liberal Protestant who believes in Hell and I'll show you a Catholic. The idea that sinners will be sent to Hell, to burn forever, doesn't jive with their idea of Jesus as all-loving and all forgiving, even though Jesus himself explicitly threatened people with Hell. So they pick and choose what they want to believe, and sweep the rest under the rug. At least the fundamentalists and Catholics take the whole package. They don't pick and choose."

Matthew nodded. "I agree with that."

They were silent for a moment.

"Let me ask you this," he said. "Are you a solo wiccan, or are you in a coven?"

"A coven."

He nodded again. "That's cool."

"There's that word again."

"Sorry about that."

She smiled.

"Umm, listen," he said. He paused for a moment. "Would it be okay if I went with you sometime to one of your coven meetings?" He was surprised by his own question.

She shook her head. "No."

"Why?" he asked.

"Well for two reasons. First, we don't accept males. We went down that road before, and it just didn't work. Especially when one of the male phonies raped one of the women. Second, we don't take observers. We're not a reality TV show. We only accept wiccans who've first followed the solo path, sincerely, and then are recommended by one of the coven members."

"Oh," he said.

"Sorry. Those are the rules. Anyway, why would you even want to come? You said you're an atheist, and we're not atheists. We just have a different view of God. Actually, we believe in a number of gods."

"Frankly, I'm not really sure. I'm an atheist, but there's some kind of void in me. I don't know. Something's missing, I guess. I'm sort of floundering around, and I'm not sure if it's just my illness, or if it maybe goes beyond that."

A look of compassion came over her. "Well, I hope you find out."

"Yeah. Me too," he said. He stood up. "I enjoyed our conversation."

She smiled. "I did too. Who knows, maybe someday you'll become a wiccan."

"Who knows," he said. He stood there looking at her.

"Here," she said. She took off her pentacle necklace and held it out to him. "Take this."

He was incredulous. "What? Really?" he said, even as he took it from her.

"Really. It's just a cheap one, no big deal. But maybe it will come to mean something to you some day. Or maybe it won't. In any case, I hope you find your way to whatever it is you're looking for."

Matthew was genuinely touched. "Thank you," he said. "Thank you very much. That's very kind of you."

"Yeah, it is, she said," and she smiled. "Now, leave me alone so I can get back to my writing. Otherwise I'll have to turn you into a parakeet or something."

He laughed. "I'm outta here." He left her and went back to his chair and his book. Every few minutes, he's stop reading and look at the pentacle. Then a kind of chill passed through him. He wondered what the hell he was doing with a pentacle in his hand.

At the morning community meeting a few days later, Matthew noticed a new addition to the unit, or more precisely, her breasts, which were huge. She was a blond woman, probably around forty years old, with a terrific figure—and those magnificently large and well-shaped breasts, no-doubt surgically built. When breakfast was served, he saw her sitting by herself, and asked if could share her table. She nodded, and he sat down.

Neither of them spoke for a while, or even looked at each other. Finally, he said, "My name is Matthew. What's yours?"

She looked up at him. "Anne," she said.

There was another silence. Then Matthew said, "I know it's hard when you first come onto the unit. If you need any help, or just somcone to talk to besides counselors and therapists, please feel free to come to me."

"Thank you," she said. "But I've been here before."

"Oh." Another long silence. "You don't have to answer this, because I know it's none of my business, really, but can I ask what brings you here?"

She took a sip of coffee and eyed him for a moment as if trying to determine his motives. Then she said, "The short answer is that I took 300 barbituates and wound up in the E.R. The long answer is that I've been struggling with depression off and on for years, and nothing—not the doctors, not the therapists, not the medications—has been able to help me. So I tried to end it, and unfortunately I was found, and so here I am."

He thought for a moment that she might cry, but she didn't. "I know where you're coming from," he said. "I'm here because I too tried to kill myself. I've been fighting depression, and nothing has helped me either. So here I am, just like you."

She stared at him for a moment. "How long have you been here?" she asked.

"Two weeks, I guess."

"If you were released today, would you kill yourself?"

"Ummm, good question." He thought for a moment. "No, I don't think I would. But a month from now, who knows?"

"So has this place helped you?"

"It has helped me, but mostly because of the other patients. I've never been around so many tortured but gentle, kind and honest people. Sometimes I think the crazy people are out on the streets, and the sane people are in here, because they can't deal with the insanity outside."

She smiled at this.

"Hey, I got you to smile," he said. "See what I mean? Fellow patients are the best therapy you can get."

They both ate in silence for a while. Then she stood up and looked at him. "Thank you, Matthew."

"It was nice to meet you, Anne. Like I said, if you feel like talking, or just need a shoulder to cry on, let me know. I'm in room 112."

"Thank you," she said, and walked away.

Matthew felt bad for her. She was obviously still in a very bad place, unhappy to be here and even more unhappy to be alive. He knew exactly how she felt.

Over the next few days Matthew had several conversations with Anne, sometimes in the dining room, sometimes in the common room. He was genuinely trying to help her, to be a friend, despite the undercurrent of lust he felt for her. He couldn't help that part; she was just so attractive. He compensated for these feelings by being a perfect gentleman, and focusing on being a friend.

A few more days passed. It was Saturday night, and the staff allowed the patients to watch a rented movie on the TV in the common room. Matthew intentionally happened to sit on the couch next to Anne. There was one other person to the left of Anne. It was cool in the room, and the three of them shared a blanket over their laps. The room was dark, except for the nurses' station at the back and the glow of the TV. The movie was a boring romantic comedy, but it was still a treat to have a normal sort of evening that one might have at home. The staff even provided popcorn, which he thought was a very nice touch.

Then, at some point in the film, Matthew felt Anne's hand on his thigh. He was stunned, and a thrill went through his body. Very slowly, without looking away from the movie, he slid his hand over hers and twined his fingers with hers. He left it there for the rest of the movie. When it was over, he looked at her and squeezed her hand. Then everyone separated and went to their rooms or to the nurses' station for nighttime meds. "Goodnight, Anne," he said. "I hope you have sweet dreams."

She smiled at him. "You too, Matthew. Goodnight."

Matthew fairly skipped to his room. She had come on to him. He couldn't believe it. As he went to sleep that night, all he could think about was her hand on his thigh, and his hand on hers, their fingers intertwined. He wondered where this could lead. Then he fell asleep.

The following day, a Sunday, was essentially a free day on the unit. Only a couple of group meetings; visitors able to come all afternoon, and some of the patients out on passes for the day. In the early evening, Matthew went into one of the phone booths to leave a message for Dr. Mendel. Suddenly Anne slipped into the booth and kissed him passionately on the lips. His knees nearly buckled. Before he could say anything, she was gone. Matthew's heart was aflutter. He was stunned. He was also very happy. He composed himself and stepped out of the booth, looking for her, but she was gone. He didn't see her again the rest of the night, but all he could think of was her. He was tempted to go to her room, on the off chance that her roommate wasn't there, but decided against it and retired to his own room. He was temporarily without a roommate, which was nice. A room to himself. As he lay in bed trying to sleep, he was tortured by thoughts of Anne, of that kiss, and he became aroused. He made himself come, in between checks, before going to sleep.

The next day, Monday, he couldn't wait to see Anne. He sat next to her at community meeting, and across from her at breakfast. He sat next to her at the first therapy group as well. There was a little free time just before lunch, so Matthew went to his room to read for a few minutes. His door was partly open. He heard a knock, and Anne's voice. "Matthew? May I come in?"

"Anne. Yes. Please do." He was thrilled.

She came in and closed the door. That was a no-no on the unit: men and women could not be in a patient room together unless the door was open. And he knew she knew it, which added to the thrill. He sat on the edge of his bed. Anne didn't say anything. She just approached him and knelt down on the floor between his legs. He felt a surge of blood into his penis. She rested her arms on his thighs and looked up at him.

"Matthew," she said. "Do you ever have dreams about sex?"

Matthew swallowed hard. He couldn't believe what he'd just heard. "Umm, yes. I do." He flushed. "Sometimes they're so realistic that I wake up having an orgasm. A wet dream, I guess you'd call it." He was amazed that he was speaking of this as if he was discussing the weather.

"I have those dreams, too," she said. "They torture me. And last night I had one about you. I woke up so horny I couldn't go back to sleep. All I could think about was you, touching you, making love to you."

"Oh, god," Matthew said. He was flabbergasted. "Anne, you have no idea how much I've thought of you. I made myself come last night just thinking about you."

She smiled. "You did?"

"Yes, I did."

"And what exactly did you think about?"

He smiled. "That's privileged information. You tell me first. What were you thinking about me?"

She didn't even hesitate. "I thought about having your cock in my mouth. I thought about you fucking me from behind."

Matthew blushed at her frankness.

"Come on," she said. "I told you, now you have to tell me."

He swallowed hard. He ran his fingers through his hair. "Okay. I thought about my cock between your breasts, about shooting cum all over them. There. I said it. Are you happy?"

"Mmm. Yes. Very."

Their eyes locked for a long moment. No smiles, no words. Anne ran her hands up and down his thighs, then rubbed her breasts across them. She stood up, and looking down into his eyes, said, "Sometimes dreams come true."

Matthew just looked up at her, speechless.

She turned and left the room. He fell back on his bed and took a deep breath. He wondered if this was really happening.

He didn't have to wait long for the answer. That night, when no one was looking, she silently took him by the hand and led him into a restroom in the back hall of the unit. She was wearing a long, pink terry cloth robe. She locked the door, then opened her robe and let it drop to the floor. She was completely naked, and her breasts seemed even larger than in his fantasies. He got an almost instant erection as she kissed him. Already she was breathing heavily. She pulled away, then bent down over the sink. "Fuck me," she said.

He placed his hands on her hips and pushed himself deep inside her wetness and began thrusting in and out. As he continued, she was stifling urges to cry out. Suddenly she turned around and sat down on the toilet cover. She pulled him toward her, and took him in her mouth, her hands cupping his buttocks. She took him deep into her throat, flicking her tongue under the shaft of his penis, driving him mad. He started panting heavily and felt himself about to come. She pulled her head away, and taking his penis in her hand, pressed it against her breasts and began pumping him.

"Oh god," he said. "Oh god."

"Come on me, baby," she said. "Come all over my tits, just like you dreamed." At that he groaned and pearly lines of semen sprang up all over her breasts and the hair on her shoulders. When he was spent he almost collapsed. "Oh god, Anne," was all he could say.

She cupped her breasts and rubbed his semen all over them. She smiled up at him. "Boy, you were loaded. You liked that, didn't you?"

He just stood there, panting heavily, and finally managed a smile. He nodded.

"We'd better get out of here before they come looking," she said.

He nodded again, and backed away, unable to speak. He pulled up his pants while she quickly wiped her hair and breasts with her robe, and put it back on.

"I'll go out first," she said, "and you follow a minute later." She kissed him. "Goodnight, Matthew. Sweet dreams."

He smiled and finally spoke. "Thank you," he said.

She kissed him again, then opened the door and left.

He waited a minute, then opened the door and stepped out into the hall. A nurse was coming down the hall, and in his guilty, breathless state he imagined that she knew exactly what was going on. He lowered his eyes and continued on to his room.

The next day, during a group therapy meeting at which Matthew was the only male, a woman began talking about her promiscuity, how she used sex with an endless stream of men as a way of hiding from, or coping with, her emotional problems. Another woman, a very large, heavy woman, interrupted her and told her she was just using that as an excuse to be a whore, and that she ought to be ashamed of herself. Suddenly, Anne, who was sitting next to Matthew, broke down, crying, her tears falling like rain. Matthew felt helpless and sad, and placed his hand on her back. She got up and left the room. He excused himself and followed her into the hallway. "Anne," he said.

She stopped and turned. He walked up to her and took her in his arms. She began sobbing. "Let me take you to your room," he said. "Why don't you just go to sleep for a while, take a little nap."

She nodded, and he walked her to her room. He stopped at the doorway. She turned and looked at him. "Please hold me," she said. "Just for a minute."

He knew he shouldn't do this, but he couldn't say no to her when she needed some companionship this way. He stepped into the room, closing the door behind him.

She laid down on the bed, on her side, and raised her arms to him. He climbed over her and laid down, his body spooned against her from behind, his arm first around her waist, then cupping her breast. He nuzzled his face into her hair and her neck. She reached back and placed her hand on the side of his face. He wished they could remain like this forever.

Just then a nurse walked in. Matthew quickly sat up.

"Matthew," she said sharply. "You know the rules. Please go to your own room."

Feeling like a naughty child, he climbed over Anne, stood up and walked meekly to his room. He laid down on his bed and thought about Anne. He just wanted to hold her, stroke her hair, do something to make her feel better. He wanted to help her.

About an hour later the head nurse came into his room. He sat up in bed. "Matthew, we've discharged Anne from the unit."

He was stunned. "What? But why?"

"We know what's been going on, and you know the rules. So did she."

"But why her? Why are you punishing her, sending her away when she's sick? Why not me?" He felt the blood rushing to his face.

"Because she was the instigator, and as long as she's here, you'll continue to break the rules."

"I know I broke the rules. But why are you punishing her, and not me? I don't understand. Why just her, and not me?"

"Because she's been here three times in two months, and this is the third time this has happened. Three strikes and you're out. She was warned about it, and she knew the consequences. This is a hospital, not her private dating service."

Matthew didn't know what to say. He just stared at the nurse. She turned and left the room, closing the door behind her. He laid down, and thought about Anne. The little bit of joy that had come into his life had been ruthlessly torn away. He started crying.

Like a reflexive response to pain, the urge to kill himself surfaced once again, like a hideous creature from the blackest depths. He didn't dwell on it. He just decided to do it. He only needed to figure out how. He looked around the room, and saw a pair of pants draped over his chair. A noose. A noose which could be hung from the top of a door. He went into the bathroom, and flung the pants legs over the top of the door, pulling them up from the other side so that the crotch of the pants would be high enough to keep his feet off the floor. He went back in and pulled the door shut. It had worked. The pants legs were firmly caught in the slight space between the top of the door and the doorframe. He locked the door, then stepped up on the toilet seat. With one arm stretched out propping himself from the door, he slipped the crotch of the pants around his neck. He let himself fall back against the door, one leg dangling, the other barely on the toilet seat, just his toe keeping him from hanging. And then, with one slight move of a muscle separating him from death, he felt doubt creeping in. Did he really want to do this? Long minutes went by, and he didn't move.

Suddenly there was a loud knock at the door. He heard the equally loud voice of one the male counselors. "Matthew! Are you in there? Matthew!"

Without thought Matthew let his toe off the toilet seat and felt his leg slam back against the door at the same moment he felt a drop and an unbearable choking and his face feeling as if it would explode. Suddenly the door opened and he collapsed to the floor. He'd forgotten that the door lock was not really a lock and could be opened from the outside. The counselor had seen the pants legs hanging from the top of the door. Matthew staggered to his feet. One of the female nurses appeared behind Dave, his rescuer.

Matthew saw consternation and concern on Dave's face. "Are you all right?" Dave asked.

Matthew was rubbing his throat. He nodded, and cleared his throat. "Yes. I'm okay. I was only hanging for an instant.

Then he saw anger creeping into Dave's expression. "That was a damn foolish thing to do, Matthew."

"I know."

"Why didn't come to one of us for help if you were struggling with thoughts of suicide?"

Matthew shook his head. "I did it on impulse. I never struggled with the thought. I just got up and did it."

"You know you're gonna have to be put on twenty-four hour watch in the quiet room."

"I know," he said, and hung his head.

He was forced to exchange his clothes for a johnny, and was taken immediately to the so-called quiet room, which was really an isolation chamber. It was at the end of the hall, and had no bathroom or any furniture at all except for a mattress on the floor in the middle of the room. There were no blankets or sheets on the mattress, and no pillowcase on the pillow. There were two cameras mounted on the ceiling, along with a bank of bright florescent lights. There was a large observation window next to the door, and a chair just outside the door where one of the staff would be sitting at all times, to keep an eye on him. He was told that if he needed to go to the bathroom, he would have to knock on the door, and the staff member on watch would escort him to a nearby restroom and escort him back when he was finished. He was a bit surprised at the Spartan arrangements, yet he understood the necessity. Still, when it was bed-time on the unit, he was unhappy to discover that the harsh lights in his room would not be turned off, nor would he be given a sheet or blanket. His hospital johnny was his only protection from the cool breeze that came from the air conditioning vents. As he laid there on the bed, he stared at one of the cameras, and wondered if someone was staring back at him from mission control, or wherever the camera's feed went. He felt like a bug.

After a fitful night of sleep, he woke in the pre-dawn hours. He knocked at the door and asked the attending nurse if he could go to the kitchen to make a cup of instant coffee. She told him that he could not go anywhere outside his room except to the bathroom, and perhaps, if it was agreed by the staff, to the common room for a limited time.

"But what about meals?" he asked.

"You'll take your meals in here or, again, if it is decided by the staff, in the common area."

"But why?" he asked. "Why can't I eat in the dining room?"

"Because there are items there that can be used to harm yourself."

"What, plastic forks?"

"Look," she said. "You put yourself in this situation. We didn't impose it on you for no reason, just to piss you off. You tried to kill yourself in your room, and it's our job as care-givers to make sure you don't try it again. I'm sorry if you don't like the restrictions, but we're doing this because we want you to survive. It may seem a bit draconian, but it's your own survival and well-being that is driving this. We're not out to get you, or tick you off. I mean, do you really think we enjoy keeping you in here and sitting outside your door twenty-four hours a day?"

Matthew looked at the floor. "I'm sorry. I don't mean to give you a hard time. It's just hard to get used to this. I feel like I'm in a fishbowl."

"Well, I'm sorry to say, but that's the idea. You need to be watched at all times, because you tried to kill yourself, and we don't want that to happen again. We're doing what we have to do to ensure your safety."

Matthew, still looking at the floor, nodded. "I know. I understand that." He was quiet for a moment. Then he looked at the nurse. "But can't I at least get a cup of coffee? What's the harm in that?"

"You know very well that the coffee and tea in the kitchen is decaffeinated, so what's the point?"

He looked at her. "Yeah, I know, and I just can't understand that. It's hard enough being in this unit. Why deny us such a small pleasure? Is caffeine supposed to be some dangerous drug that will drive patients to suicide or something? It's ridiculous."

"Look. I don't make the rules, okay? My job is to enforce them. I'm quite sure that these rules weren't instituted just to torture patients. This is a hospital, not a prison."

"Can I at least have my books? I promise not to try to kill myself with papercuts."

The nurse gave him a slight smile. "Okay. I'll see to it that your books are returned to you later on.

"Thank you," he said, truly appreciative.

"Can I also have my CD player?"

She shook her head. "I'm sorry, but you can't have that."

"Why not?"

"Because it has a power cord, and a cord for the headphone. Do I need to spell it out?"

Matthew looked at the floor again. "No."

They were both silent for a moment.

"How long do I have to stay in here?" he asked.

"That's really up to you. As long as the medical staff believes you are at risk of harming yourself, you'll have to remain here."

"Well, what if I put on a good act? How would they know?"

"Look," she said. "If you really want to kill yourself, you'll find a way. But we want to make it as difficult as possible for you to do that. We've had patients kill themselves in ways no one could have foreseen, but we can only do our best to prevent those things from happening. We're not your enemy. We're trying to help you, and keep you alive."

Matthew nodded, and didn't say anything. A wave of misery suddenly crashed over him and he started to cry. He didn't know why, but he knew it had nothing to do with coffee. The nurse left him alone, and he retreated to the mattress, curling into a fetal position, sobbing. He didn't understand, but it didn't matter. Misery was broad enough to encompass every reason. Beneath the harsh glare of the fluorescent lights, he slipped back into a fitful sleep.

Later that morning he was awakened by another nurse, and she told him that a doctor would be by shortly to talk to him. He sat up for a moment, but with nowhere to go or nothing to put on, he laid back on the mattress. A few minutes later, a tall, dark-haired doctor about his own age came into the room, and Matthew sat up again. The doctor exuded a kind of warmth that put Matthew at ease.

"Hi, Matthew."

"Hi, doctor."

"How are you feeling this morning?"

"Miserable."

"Are you having any thoughts of hurting yourself?"

Matthew shook his head. "No. It seems to have gone out of my system for now."

The doctor nodded. "That's good."

There was a moment of silence.

"Listen, Matthew. Are you familiar with ECT?"

"ECT? You mean shock treatments?"

"Electro convulsive therapy," he said.

"Right," Matthew said. "Shock treatments."

"Matthew, it's not what you think it is. It isn't some sort of mind erasing torture. You would be unconscious through the whole procedure. You would be given two or three treatments each week for several weeks. The results are very impressive. Most patients have a marked improvement—a marked relief from depression—after just a few sessions."

Matthew didn't say anything, but the thought of some sort of relief appealed to him.

"We have a video that explains ECT in great detail, and shows the actual procedure. We can arrange for you to see it in the common room, with a staff member. Would you like to see it?"

"Yes."

"Good. I'll talk to the staff and we'll set it up for you."

Matthew nodded.

"Is there anything you'd like to talk about? Can you tell me what triggered your suicide attempt?"

"It wasn't premeditated; it was just an impulsive act. I was miserable."

"But what were your thoughts before that impulse? Do you remember if anything caused it? I understand that you had some sort of relation with one of the female patients, and that she was discharged as a result. Is that what triggered you?"

"Yes, I guess . . . well, I know that upset me a lot. And that's what I was thinking about just before I acted. So I guess that's what triggered me. I was just really upset. I was angry, and I also felt really bad about what happened to Anne. And the next thing I knew I was putting the pants over the door."

"Okay," the doctor said. "But you're not having thoughts now about harming yourself?"

Matthew shook his head. "No, I'm not. And I regret what I did yesterday. It was stupid."

"Can you contract with me that if you start having those thoughts again that you'll talk to one of the staff?"

"Yes. I'll contract with you."

"Okay, good," the doctor said. "I'll check in with you again this afternoon."

"Thank you, doctor."

The doctor left, and Matthew laid down again.

A short time later one of the nurses came in with his books.

"Thank you," he said, taking the books.

"Doctor Weld said that you wanted to see the ECT video?"

"Yes, I do."

"Okay, well, we've got it out in the common room if you'd like to see it now."

"Yes. I'd like to."

He got up and followed her out of the room into the common area. There were a few other patients sitting around, and they all looked at him as he came in. Most of them gave him a smile or a compassionate look. "Hi, Matthew," a woman said. Matthew managed a return smile. The nurse reached up to the TV mounted on the wall, and put in the tape. He sat down, and the nurse sat down near him.

He watched the video with intense interest and liked what he saw, especially the part where they showed the actual procedure being administered to a patient. He'd expected to see the patient's body convulsing from the electrical charge, but only his foot was moving, almost in a circular fashion, rather than in uncontrolled spasms. By the end of the video he was relieved and convinced that he wanted to have the treatment. He said so to the nurse.

"I'm glad, Matthew," she said. "It might really help you."

"At this point, I'll try anything."

"I'll tell the doctor."

Matthew nodded. "Do I have to go back to the room now?"

"I'm afraid so," she replied.

Matthew got up, and the nurse followed him to his room. He sat down on the mattress as the nurse closed the door, and was glad to see his books. He rolled onto his stomach, propped *Being and Nothingness* on the pillow and began to read. It felt good to escape into the dense words. He read for a couple of hours, then napped for a while.

He was wakened a few hours later by Dr. Weld. "How are you doing, Matthew?"

"Okay."

"Any thoughts of harming yourself?"

Matthew shook his head. "No. None at all."

The doctor noticed the Sartre book. A look approaching disapproval crossed his face. "That's some heavy duty reading you've got there. A bit grim, isn't it?"

"Maybe it is, but I'm a bit grim myself. It matches my mood. Just like rainy days."

The doctor looked at the book again, but didn't say anything.

"Did the nurse tell you that I've decided to go ahead with the ECT treatments?"

"Yes, she did," he replied. "I'm glad that you decided to do it. I think it might help you."

"Well, at this point, I'll try anything."

"We're not going to waste any time with this. I'm arranging to have your first treatment tomorrow morning."

Matthew felt a twinge of fear, despite what he saw in the video. "Okay," he said.

"As you saw in the video, it's a very innocuous procedure. Quite different from the popular misconception."

Matthew nodded.

"The treatment will be administered downstairs in the basement. It will be very early, around six. A nurse will come and bring you down."

"Okay," Matthew said.

The doctor smiled. "You'll be pleased to know that I'm going to lift the ban on your restriction now. This will remain your room for the time being, but you're free to go about the unit whenever you want, including the dining room. But first I want you to contract with me again that you won't try to harm yourself. Can you make that promise?"

"Yes, I promise doctor." He extended his hand and they shook on it.

"Very good," the doctor said. "I'll see you tomorrow."

"Thank you, Doctor."

The doctor left. Matthew was pleased. He picked up his book and went out to the common room. The other patients smiled to see him come in without an escort. He smiled in return and dropped into a chair. It felt good to be free again. He opened his book and resumed his reading. But a moment later he decided to exercise his new-found freedom, and went to the kitchen to make a cup of instant decaf coffee. Despite its bitter taste, it was one of the most appreciated cups of coffee he'd ever had.

Later that day he started asking around the unit for any patients who might have had, or were now having, ECT treatments. Their responses did not please him, and he began to wonder if he was doing the right thing.

Chapter Six

Matthew was brought back to a regular room the morning after his first treatment. Despite his headache and disorientation, he was very glad to be a regular patient again.

Matthew spent several more weeks in the hospital, and other than his treatments, they were uneventful. After a half-dozen treatments, he began to feel a slight improvement in his mood, and he was hopeful that the ECT might really help him. But as the treatments continued, the improvement leveled off. He was deeply disappointed. And he was also becoming very tired of being in the hospital. He wanted to go home. In order to expedite this, he lied to the doctors and nurses about his mood. He told them he was feeling better and better, and put on an act to demonstrate his great improvement. After a dozen treatments, he was released from the hospital. He was still terribly depressed, but his discharge pleased him. He was free again. When he walked into his apartment, the first thing he did was pour himself four fingers of bourbon, and proceeded to get hammered.

Unlike everything else, Matthew's libido was oddly unaffected by his depression, and a few days later he was at it again. It was late afternoon and he was sitting in the café area of a Barnes and Noble bookstore. He saw a girl walk up and get in line. She looked even younger than Jenna, maybe just out of high school. She was wearing large, hip sunglasses; her dark hair was stylishly coifed, and she had on an unbearably short denim skirt, along with high heels. Her legs were long, smooth and tanned. His lust fired up like an engine. She flipped through a copy of *Vogue* Magazine as she stood in line, and Matthew couldn't take his eyes off of her. She looked up from the magazine, and looked around the café. Her sunglasses were light enough that he could see her eyes, and her gazed stopped on him. She held his gaze for a moment, then went back to her magazine. As she continued to wait, she looked up several times, and each time she made eye contact with him. Matthew felt the familiar electricity surging through him. She bought a cup of coffee, then walked over to the station where the cream and sugar was. She glanced over at him again. As she was leaving, she walked right past his table, and though she didn't look at him then, just before exiting the café area, she looked over her shoulder right at him. Matthew was convinced she was waiting to be plucked from the tree. He got up and followed her from the café. He kept his distance at first, watching her as she went to the magazine aisle. He stopped at the other end of the aisle, and started flipping through a sports magazine, pretending he was interested, but looking over every few moments hoping to catch her eye. Finally, she looked his way, and gave him a slight smile. That was all he needed. He moved down the aisle until he was standing only a few feet away from her. He took a magazine from the rack, then looked at her. "I hope you don't mind my being so forward," he said, "but I just have to tell you that you are an extraordinarily beautiful woman."

She smiled at him. "Thank you," she said.

"You look like a model from that magazine you're reading."

She gave a small laugh. "I try."

"Well, you've definitely succeeded."

"Thank you," she said again.

Matthew looked around for a moment. "Umm, can I buy you a cup of coffee? No, wait, that was stupid, you just bought one," he said, shaking his head.

She smiled again.

"Can I buy you a fashion magazine, instead?"

"Are you trying to pick me up?"

Matthew flushed. "Well . . . yes. I guess I am."

She put the magazine back on the rack.

"I'm Matthew," he said.

"Maria," she said.

"Maria? I've always liked that name."

"I think it's kind of old fashioned, but that's the name they gave me."

"Well, I like it," he said. "Umm . . . listen. If you're not doing anything, would you like to go out for a drive with me? I have a Jaguar, and it's quite beautiful. You can even drive it, if you'd like."

"A Jaguar, huh? That's pretty cool. Sure. I'll go for a ride."

He was surprised that he'd picked her up so easily. Obviously, he thought, she was looking to be picked up. He was doubly surprised because he was practically twice her age. But maybe, he thought, she's the kind that goes for older men and money and expensive cars, rather than pimply, slovenly boys her own age with their pants around their knees. As they left the store, he opened the door for her and gently placed his hand on her back as she went through. A thrill ran up his arm. He walked her to his car. "What do you think?" he said.

She looked at it from end to end, and nodded. "It's gorgeous," she said.

"Yeah, she is. Just like you." He was a little embarrassed by his tacky remark. "Would you like to drive it?"

"No. I'll let you drive."

He opened the door for her, and as she got in his eyes lingered on her long legs. He closed the door, then went around and got in.

"It's beautiful," she said, looking around the interior.

"I agree," he said. "Listen. Have you eaten yet? Can I take you out to dinner?"

"Sure. That would be great."

"Do you like fine Italian? I know of a very nice place we could go. The food and service are excellent."

"Sure. I love Italian. I'm Italian myself."

"Oh, perfect," he said, putting the car in gear. As they were leaving the parking lot, he came out with another corny line. "I've heard that Italians are very passionate. Is that true?"

She smiled, without looking at him. "Yes. Very," she said.

"I'm French. We French are quite passionate, too."

"Yes, I've heard that," she said. "I've always wanted to go to Paris. Rome, too. I look through magazines and books dreaming about being there, and having an affair with a handsome marquis or something."

He looked at her and smiled. "What if I told you that I'm a French marquis?"

She laughed. "Then I'd say you're a goddamned liar."

"Oh, well. I was just trying to impress you. It was worth a try."

She laughed again.

It was a short drive to the restaurant, and by sheer luck he found a parking spot right across the street. "La Dolce Vita," she said.

"Yes. Have you been here before?"

"No. But I've always wanted to try it."

"I think you'll like it. It's very nice."

He went around and opened the car door for her. They walked across the street and into the restaurant. It was an impressive, romantic place, with candles, gleaming glasses and silverware, and spotless white tablecloths. A number of heads turned to look at her, but she seemed to take it in as a matter of course. A waiter in a tuxedo led them to a table by a window, and pulled the chair out for her.

Matthew watched her as she looked about the dining room. "Well, what do you think?" he asked. "A beautiful place, huh?"

"Yes, it is," she said. She was obviously impressed.

"We could pretend we're in Rome, and that I'm a handsome French marquis. And you're a glamorous model who's been in *Vogue*, *Elle* and all the other great fashion magazines."

"And I live in Monaco."

He smiled. "Yes. You live in Monaco, and all the rich playboys invite you out on their yachts, but you always turn them down."

"That's right," she said. "I'm highly selective of the men I see."

"Well then, I'm quite honored to be escorting you this evening."

She smiled. "Yes. You should be."

"Did you see all the men practically breaking their necks to get a look at you when we came in?"

"Of course. I get that all the time. Since I was probably thirteen years old. I like it. For some reason, though, when I'm in my car, and they're in their cars, they get crude—you know, the cat calls and stuff like that. And construction sites, too. It's such a cliché. I just ignore it. But I like it, too."

Matthew was very happy and excited. This was going to be a marvelous evening. Once again, he couldn't believe he was with such a beautiful, sexy woman. A girl, really, and he was flattered that she was with him. She made him feel young.

As they looked over the menu, he suspected that she didn't really understand what some of the entrees were. He offered to explain them, hoping she wouldn't take offense, but she readily accepted the offer and asked him about a number of dishes.

"Shall I order a bottle of wine?" he asked. Then it dawned on him that she probably wasn't even old enough, legally, to drink.

"Absolutely," she said.

He picked up the wine menu. "Well, then. I think a fine Italian wine is in order here. I usually drink French wine, but in your honor I think we'll go with Italian."

She smiled. "You're sweet."

He smiled back. "I try."

He ordered the wine, and after they'd ordered their meals, they chatted while sipping the wine. She was obviously enjoying herself. He wondered if she'd ever been to a restaurant as fancy and expensive as this one. He wondered, too, if he was going to get laid. He thought his chances were good, and the mere possibility thrilled him.

During dinner, they shared some of their life stories, though Matthew was careful to steer clear of any of his psychiatric problems. He put the emphasis on his publishing career and his education, wanting to impress her, and puffed up his tastes in music, art and literature, trying to fit the image of a rich marquis.

She, on the other hand, was quite frank about her lower class background, her abusive father, her loser boyfriends, and her desire for a high class life. She also told him that her immediate goal was to open up her own beauty salon which would appeal to high-end customers, rather than the local yokels and grandmothers.

After espressos and dessert, he walked her back to the car, wondering what to do next. He saw himself from a third person point of view, and wondered what the hell this guy was doing. He was obviously out of control; he was trying to have a one night stand with a girl who was getting report cards less than a year ago. He'd succeeded in impressing her, and now he was hoping to reap the rewards by getting laid. And she was just a kid. He felt a wave of self-disgust, but as he looked at her, his disgust was buried under a larger wave of lust.

"Shall we go for a drive?" he asked, after they'd gotten into the car.

"Sure, that sounds nice."

He drove aimlessly for a while, then decided to head to the local airport, the kind of place that has a windsock, and where hours go by before a little Cessna comes in or takes off. The place would be completely dead at night, and there was a large parking lot.

After a short drive, he pulled into the dark parking lot, and cut the engine. He sat for a moment. Then he turned to her and abruptly said, "Can I kiss you?"

"Yes," she said.

He leaned over, and they kissed. Within a few moments he was running his hands over her body, following the contours of her breasts, her waste, her thighs. She placed her hand on his crotch, as if to discern if he was excited, and began messaging him through his pants. He was beginning to breathe heavily. "Let's get into the back seat," he said.

She didn't reply, but they both opened their doors and got into the back seat. He pulled her over so that she was sitting on his lap, her back to him. Her legs were open, his own legs between her thighs. He cupped her breasts, and she leaned back, turning her head over her shoulder while they kissed. He slipped his hand down between her legs, and felt the smooth fabric of her panties, with its soft mound of hair underneath. He slipped them down her legs, then struggled as he pulled his own pants down. His cock was in the vortex of her legs, and she began stroking it, up and down. Then she lifted herself up, positioned his cock under her cunt, and slid down on his shaft. Her pussy was gloriously tight. As she began moving around on him, her hips moving in slow elipses, he felt a tremendous surge, almost like fire, moving toward his groin. As his breathing grew deeper, she began moving faster, and as he raised his hips and thrust up into her as hard as he could, he groaned and felt himself erupting inside her, spurting and spurting till he thought he'd never stop.

When it did stop, he sat there running his hands slowly around her body. Though she'd moaned and gasped a lot, he wasn't sure if she'd actually come. To his surprise, he realized he didn't care. He laid down with her on the seat for a while, kissing and touching. After a while, without saying a word he sat up, and she did too. He pulled his pants up while she put her panties back on. They got out and got up into the front seats. "Thank you," he said. "That was incredible."

"Yeah, it was," she said.

They rode in silence back to the Barnes and Noble, where her car was parked.

"That's it, right there," she said. It was a red Mazda convertible. "What do you think?" she asked.

"It's you," he said.

He pulled up next to it, got out and opened the door for her. They kissed. Even though he doubted he'd ever call her, he didn't want to offend her, so he asked for her phone number. She pulled a pen and piece of paper from her purse, and wrote her number. She gave it to him, and said, "I had a great time. Maybe you really are a French marquis."

He smiled. "Maybe you really are a fashion model."

They kissed again, and he watched as she got into her car and drove off. He got into his own car and sat for a few minutes. The car smelled like sex. His euphoria began to melt away as he thought about what had just happened. She was just a kid. True, she was legal, and he hadn't had to twist her arm. She'd wanted it as much he did. But still, he felt dirty, not only because he had taken advantage of a gum-snapping teenage girl, but that he'd had another casual sexual encounter. What was next, he thought. A fifty-year old divorcee with tanned, leathery skin, dyed blond hair and tons of makeup? And yet, he had no doubt that if he could turn the clock back a few hours, he'd do it all again. So his guilt struck him as phony. He wondered what was going on. On the one hand, he felt that he was just a red-blooded American male sowing his oats, especially since he'd never sown his oats before meeting Helen. On the other hand, he thought of the woman in the group at the hospital who'd admitted to hiding her misery in an endless succession of casual sexual encounters. Was he doing the same thing? He thought about what he'd just done, screwing a teenager, and decided that he definitely was out of control again. He didn't know if he was trying to run from his problems, but something was not right. As he drove home, he fought the urge to drive his car into a tree. He wondered if he should go back to the hospital, but decided against it because he hadn't actually tried to harm himself, and besides, he'd probably just compound things by trying to score with another patient or nurse. Plus, he hated the place. The hospital wouldn't solve anything. He got back to his apartment, and to his disgust, when he got into bed, he could think of nothing but being in the backseat with Maria, and he made himself come.

For one of the only days in the past few months, Matthew went to the office. His boss seemed glad to see him, and his co-workers and employees stopped by to say hello and welcome him back. He noticed a strange look in the eyes of many, as if they were looking through glass at a strange, deformed creature on the other side.

A short while later, his boss appeared at his office door, and soberly asked if he would come to his office. Matthew instinctively felt that this was not going to be something good.

When he entered his boss's office, he was surprised, and at the same time, not surprised, to see the director of human resources, a tense, middle aged woman, sitting in the office. His boss closed the door and sat down behind his desk.

"Matthew," he said. "We know that you have been going through a rough time, a terrible time. And I hope you know, I think you know, that we've been very supportive of you, and have filled the breach until such time as you could come back and pick up where you'd left off. You were, after all, one of the finest young managers in this company."

Matthew felt the familiar knot in his stomach growing tighter by the moment.

His boss continued. "I think you know that we've gone out of our way to keep things going during your absence; but the problem is, it has gone on too long, with no real sign that you'll be returning for good. But even that isn't the real issue."

Matthew saw his boss glance at the HR director.

"Matthew, as I'm sure you well know, your performance as a manager has suffered. In fact, it's become unacceptable. It pains me to say that as much as it must pain you to hear it. But the fact is, as you well know, we're running a business here, and we cannot continue to carry a manager who is rarely here, and when he is here, makes poor decisions and expensive mistakes. As a manager, I think you well understand that."

Matthew was numb, but he nodded. "Yes. I do."

"Okay," his boss continued.

Matthew at this point was staring down at his hands, which he'd linked together.

"Well," his boss said. "We have two options here."

Matthew looked up at him.

"We could put you on a three month probation, in which case we would expect your performance to radically improve, according to explicit standards we'd set for you, which basically mirror the performance standards you'd set in the past." His boss paused for a moment. "If you choose that option, and fail to meet the required standards, we would have no choice but to fire you, with no severance package."

Matthew's throat constricted. He couldn't believe he was hearing this from the man who'd always told him he was a 'rate-buster,' someone who set new standards of performance, and was destined for high office some day.

"The other option," his boss continued, "would be to accept your resignation right now." Again he glanced over at the HR director. "If you choose this option, we will give you a severance package equal to a full year of your current salary. This would not of course have any impact on your vested pension or your salary investment plan."

Matthew gazed in silence at his boss, then looked at the HR director, who lowered her eyes. Matthew's eyes were welling up. "I'll resign," he said.

His boss looked at him sympathetically. "I think you're making the right decision, Matthew."

Matthew lowered his eyes, and did not respond.

"To make things a little easier, Vicky here has drafted a resignation letter. If it meets your approval, all you have to do is sign it."

Vicky handed Matthew the paper, and through his tear-blurred eyes, he read the brief letter. His throat was constricted. "That's fine," he managed to say.

"Good," John said. "If you'll just sign it, we'll consider it effective today."

Matthew, almost in a trance, signed the letter.

His boss looked at him for a moment. "This is hard for all of us," he said, "especially, I know, for you. But you're making the right decision."

Matthew nodded.

"Of course, we'll send you written confirmation of all this."

Matthew nodded again.

Okay," his boss said. He paused for a moment. "We'll expect you to have your office cleared by the end of the day, and all proprietary files, contracts, price lists, etcetera, turned over to me."

Matthew nodded, unable to speak. He was in a sort of numb stupor. He'd expected this day to come, yet had tried to hide this from himself.

His boss stood up, and extended his hand. Vickie stood as well.

Matthew shook his boss's hand. "I'm sorry," Matthew said.

A look of sadness came over his boss's face. "I'm sorry, too."

Matthew left the office, returned to his own office and shut the door. He decided he would not say goodbye to anyone. He couldn't handle that. He would just gather his personal effects, hand over his files, and leave.

And that's what he did. He avoided people all morning, and ignored any phone calls. Around noon he returned to his boss's office. He handed over some crucial binders, and relied on his boss's trust when he told him that the rest of the proprietary documents were intact in his office files.

His boss rose. "I'm so sorry, Matthew, that it's had to end this way." He extended his hand.

Matthew shook his hand.

"I hope," his boss said, "that you'll come by and visit us sometime, if you're feeling better."

Matthew's eyes were welling again. "I don't think I can do that," he said, and he walked out. He took his box of personal effects, and without saying goodbye to anyone, left his office during lunch hour and left the building. He couldn't bear to look back. He called for a taxi, as he didn't want to carry the heavy carton on the subway. As he sat in the back seat of the cab, he felt his eyes welling again, and his lip trembling. He decided that he would not cry; he would simply refuse to cry. But he failed, and he wept for the duration of the ride to his apartment.

He drank himself to oblivion that night, but he didn't cut himself, despite the urge, and he took this as a minor victory. In a way he was relieved that he no longer had to pretend, no longer had to pull himself together to get through a day at the office, meanwhile making serious mistakes that shamed him.

The following day, Matthew decided to escape. He needed to get out of here, to get away from everyone and everything. He needed a complete change of scenery for a few days, maybe even a week, and to be completely anonymous. He would go to Quebec City, his favorite travel destination. He considered it the most beautiful city in North America, a marvelous slice of Old France, only a day's drive from Boston. He threw some clothes and toiletry articles into a bag, got into his Jaguar and headed north. He was getting away from his life as much as he was traveling to Quebec. He needed this. It might help him to re-set the clock, regain a grip on things, maybe even heal a bit. So he drove seven hours and felt genuinely happy when he passed through the stone, copper-towered St. Louis gate into Old Quebec. It was like another world, and that was exactly what he wanted and needed.

He pulled into the garage beneath the city hall, and gambled that a room would be available at the townhouse hotel he'd stayed at before, named after one of his great grandmothers from the seventeenth century. He took his bag with him. As it turned out, there was a room available on the third floor, and he took his key and bag up the stairs. The room was as he'd expected, based on his previous stay: a high-ceilinged room with French Second Empire furniture, a marble fireplace mantle, and tapestry rugs.

He sat down on the bed, and sighed deeply. He was here. He was safe. No one could find him. Nothing bad was ahead of him; there was only Quebec

City, a place he adored, with bars, restaurants, cafes and bookstores ahead of him. And the exquisite beauty of the city. Already his spirit had lifted a little. He had done the right thing, the best thing, by coming here. It would do him much more than the ECT treatments had done to restore his mental well-being. In fact, he was thrilled.

    He enjoyed several days there practicing the few French expressions he could remember from high school, browsing in the many bookshops, pretending he could read French, but really just enjoying the experience of being in these shops and listening to the French language. He wandered the narrow and colorful streets and passed in and out of the handsome stone gates, taking pictures at seemingly every turn. He dined and went drinking in some of the countless restaurants, cafes and bars. He'd not sought any romantic encounters, despite the fact that the women in Quebec had a chic beauty that was all but absent in staid Boston. Matthew was greatly enjoying the trip, and felt the breath of life slowly, very slowly, being breathed into his lungs. His only regret about coming to Quebec was that he knew as soon as he left, as soon as he returned to his cave in Boston, it would be as if he'd never left. The thought of it made his stomach tighten.

    He decided that before returning to Boston he'd make an overnight trip up to Charlevoix, a hilly, scenic region further north on the St. Lawrence river, and stay at Le Manoir Richelieu, a magnificent turn-of-the century hotel high above the river, that looked like a chateaux from the Loire Valley in France. There was also an adjacent casino, and he was looking forward to playing the roulette wheel, his favorite casino game.

    Just before leaving the city, he decided to stop in Paillard's, a French-style boulangerie, or bakery, situated near the St. Jean gate. He parked his Jaguar on rue St. Jean and walked a short block, and as he was about to enter, he noticed a beautiful woman sitting at a table near the large window. His heart and loins stirred. He entered the café and cast a glance her way and was stunned by her appearance. She had coiffed blonde hair, a face like an angel, and a voluptuous body sheathed in a white silk blouse and skin-tight jeans. Her high-heeled shoes were hooked on the rung of the high stool she sat on, and she was reading a book with an espresso cup before her. She was so beautiful that Matthew felt something like music pass through his body. And yet there was a kind of sadness in her expression, which did not detract from her beauty, but in some strange way enhanced it. She looked up at him briefly, then returned to her reading. In that moment, looking into her eyes, he saw the sadness more deeply. Matthew was smitten. He walked to the counter, ordered a coffee to go, and as he stood at the little island counter where the cream and sugar was located, he couldn't take his eyes off her. He didn't want to seem crude or rude in staring at her but she was so beautiful that he could now hear a kind of heavenly choir in his head. She was the incarnation of the sweetest poetry, or to put it another way, she was incredibly hot. She looked to be his age, and he noted that she didn't have a wedding ring on her finger. He assumed though that a woman such as her had a boyfriend, as well as numerous prospective boyfriends waiting in the wings, ready to move in at the slightest hint of a breach in her relationship.

As he stared at her, he was electrified when she put down her book and again looked right at him. Her gaze seemed just a tad too long to be casual, and his heart leapt to his throat. But he didn't know what to do, so he added his cream and sugar, and with a last look her way, exited the café. But he couldn't bring himself to walk away. So he stood in front and lit a cigarette, his back to the café windows. After a few minutes, he gathered his courage and turned around to look at her, and was shocked to see her looking steadily right back at him. His throat constricted, and again an electric shock pass through him. He was overwhelmed, and his fight-or-flight instinct made him turn around and walk away, much to his dismay.

As he walked down the street towards his car, he felt like there were elastic cords connecting him to her, and they were stretching and becoming more taught the further he walked, yet he felt powerless to do anything but to keep walking. He reached his car, and reluctantly got behind the wheel and started the engine. He sat there for ten minutes, full of regret, and after a heavy sigh, pulled away, heading up rue St. Jean. As he negotiated the narrow streets, trying to get to the St. Louis gate and out of the city, he found himself caught in a maze of one-way streets, and soon found himself heading down a street that angled up from rue St. Jean. Suddenly, he spotted her walking up the hill, and felt the electricity again. Here was a second chance, and he had to do something. He couldn't let this extraordinary woman pass through his fingers again. He wanted to know her, to find out who she was, what she liked, what she did for a living, where she lived, and yes, to posses her. He wanted to be with her in some way, any way. He couldn't just drive by without making an effort, so, as he approached her, he slowed and pressed the button to open the passenger-side window. He knew instinctively that she was Quebecois, not an American tourist, so he spoke some of the few French words he knew.

"Excusez moi," he said leaning toward the window.

She stopped and looked at him, and he was sure he saw a spark of recognition in her eyes.

He faced the double hex of thinking of something to say to her, and then somehow communicating to her in his broken French. "J'ai vous regarder dans la Boulangerie Palliard; puis je vous donnez un . . . un . . ." he didn't know to say "ride" in French. In desperation he said, "Parlez vous anglais?"

"Oui . . . Yes," she said. "Are you lost?"

"Well, sort of," he said.

To his delight, she came over to his car and looked in the window. "Where are you trying to go?" she asked, in her delightful French accent.

"Well, I'm going to Charlevoix," he said, "but I'm having trouble getting out of the city, with all the walls and one-way streets."

She arched her lovely eyebrows. "Charlevoix? What's an American like you venturing to Charlevoix for? That's reserved for the Quebecois, a place to escape from you tourists."

He laughed through his excitement and her immediate knowledge that he was American. "Pouvez vous aidez moi?" He was proud of his French sentence.

"Oui," she said, "I'll show you."

Then she shocked him by opening the door. He saw her high heel, then her perfect leg, and then her whole miraculous body coming into the car, and then she was sitting next to him. He couldn't believe it. His heart was pounding a hole through his rib cage. "Merci," was all he could muster. He stared at her for a moment. Was this really happening?

"Go to the top of this hill," she said, "and make a right."

For the next few minutes he tried to concentrate on following her directions and, in his distracted state, not running over the many pedestrians that crowded the sidewalks and streets. Then he saw the St. Louis gate, and knew that passing through it would lead him out of the old city and towards the highway interchanges. He was grateful, and wanted to offer her a ride to wherever she'd been headed.

"Can I give you a ride anywhere?" he asked, looking at her.

"Yes. Charlevoix would be nice," she said.

He almost choked. "Charlevoix? You want to go to Charlevoix with me?" He felt as if a kind of dreamy unreality was settling around him.

"Sure. Why not? I'm not doing anything, and you seem like a nice fellow. Plus, you're quite handsome. I'm willing to take the chance that you're not a serial killer or rapist."

Again, his throat constricted. "No, I'm not, I promise you. And you're quite beautiful yourself, if I may say so."

"Of course you may say so," she said, and gave a cute little laugh.

As they drove west out of the city, the traffic and maze of highway interchanges drew his concentration, but she directed him as only a native could. Soon they were on the highway leading northeast from the city, paralleling the St. Lawrence. He began to relax, reveling in the fact that this woman he'd seen in the boulangerie was now sitting beside him on his way to Charlevoix. He wondered why and how this gorgeous woman could be here, riding in a car with a total stranger. For a moment he considered that she might be a hooker, but quickly dispensed with the idea. It just didn't fit with this person sitting beside him. But he wanted to know who she was, and what she wanted. He wanted to know everything about her.

"Would you like to make a little side excursion on the way?" she asked. "It's just over that bridge up ahead. It's the Ile d'Orlean, and I think you'll like it. It's very scenic."

"Sure, that would be great," he said. "I've heard of it, and seen it on the maps."

"Do you like wine?"

A thrill went through him. "I love wine. Why do you ask?"

"There's a lovely vineyard there, and their wine is surprisingly good."

"That sounds wonderful," he said. "I wouldn't have imagined that an island in the middle of the St. Lawrence River would be producing wine."

"In the seventeenth century it was referred to as the Isle of Bacchus because of its wild grapes."

They turned off the highway and crossed over the long, high suspension bridge which connected the island with the north bank of the river. They came to a small crossroads, and she told him to turn left. They drove a ways along a scenic road. Then she said, "There it is, on the left up ahead."

"Okay, I see the sign." He slowed and turned onto a dirt road that rose gradually between endless rows of grapevines. At the top of the hill a beautiful pair of buildings came into view. They were stone, painted white, with blue-framed windows, and vines hanging down over the walls.

"Man, this looks like something out of Bordeaux," he said.

He parked the car in front of one of the small buildings, and they got out. A chocolate-haired dog approached, tail wagging, and Matthew petted him. "Okay, buddy, where do we go to buy some wine?" He looked up and saw a small wooden sign pointing to a path between the two buildings. At the same moment the dog turned and headed down the path, as if he'd understood Matthew's question. He looked at Claire and smiled. "Now that's a well trained dog."

Claire smiled, but didn't say anything. She followed Matthew and the dog down the path.

At the bottom of the path, to the left, Matthew spotted a door at the back of one of the buildings. A carved bunch of purple grapes graced the door. The dog walked to the door and looked up at Matthew, tail wagging. Matthew was seriously intrigued by the dog's leadership. He opened the door for Claire, and they walked into a small area which opened onto rooms filled with wine racks from which protruded the necks of countless wine bottles. A stocky man with a warm, tanned face came in and greeted them in French. Claire and he exchanged a few words in French which Matthew did not understand, except for the word "American." The vintner went into one of the side-rooms, and returned with several bottles of white wine. He opened one of them and poured some into two small wine glasses.

Matthew and Claire tasted the wine, and they both smiled. "C'est bon," Matthew said, trying to act the enlightened visitor. "J'ai deux, s'il vous plait."

The vintner looked puzzled, and looked at Claire. "Deux bouteilles, s'il vous plait," she said.

Matthew looked at Claire and laughed. "Right. Like I said. Two bottles."

Claire shook her head. "You tourists are so helpless."

"Ah, that's where you're wrong," he said. He pulled a French phrase book out of his pocket. "See this? I can handle any situation in fluent French, because this book has all the necessary phrases in phonetic spellings." He laughed.

Claire laughed, too. "Except how to order two bottles."

The vintner put two bottles into a paper bag, and Matthew paid him. He asked Claire to ask him if he had any plastic cups. Claire said a few words, and the vintner smiled, disappeared into one of the rooms and came back with two plastic wine glasses.

Matthew grinned. "Merci beaucoup," he said, taking the glasses.

The vintner smiled again, and said something in French which he didn't understand. Matthew opened the door for Claire and they walked back to the car, again accompanied by the friendly dog.

As soon as they got into the car, Claire pulled a bottle out of the bag. "Well, what are you waiting for?" she said.

Matthew grinned. "Un moment, s'il vous plait." He got out, opened the trunk, and pulled a corkscrew out of a bag of tools and supplies. He got back into the car, uncorked the bottle, and poured both of them a generous amount of wine. "To a wonderful day and night," he said.

"To a wonderful day and night," she said, smiling.

They both drank deeply. Matthew refilled the glasses, then started the engine and pulled out of the parking area and back to the road. They drove back over the high-arched bridge, and back onto the road heading north to Charlevoix. They continued to drink as he drove, and he noticed that Claire's mood was brightening. She became more animated, talkative, and showed her beautiful smile more often. Matthew himself felt a pleasant mix of giddiness and relaxation. He wanted to be nowhere else but exactly where he was right now. It was as if the past and future had melted away, leaving only this ongoing, perfect moment. As they continued on their way, a huge gothic church, like a European cathedral, came into view on the right, close to the river. "Wow," he said. "That's magnificent."

"St. Anne de Beaupre," she said. "It is beautiful, isn't it? You should see the interior. It's stunningly beautiful. People from around the world make pilgrimages there. John Paul II visited once."

"It's really something," Matthew said. A few moments later the church was out of sight, behind them.

As they continued north toward Charlevoix, they finished the bottle of wine. Matthew felt wonderful. "Shall we crack open the second bottle?" he asked, hoping she would say yes.

She smiled. "That would be a 'oui.'" Matthew pulled into the first parking area, opened the bottle, and filled their glasses.

"Let's swap wine," she said.

"I don't understand. What do you mean?"

"Uh. You're so naïve," she said, shaking her head. "I'll drink some wine, hold it in my mouth, and then we'll kiss. I'll push the wine into your mouth for you to drink. Then you return the favor."

Matthew felt a thrill pass through his body. He felt like he was in some sort of sweet dream.

Claire took a long sip for her glass. They leaned in and kissed, and Matthew thrilled at the sensation of the warm wine coming into his mouth from between her soft lips. He swallowed, and grinned as he pulled away. "Oh my god," he said. "That felt so good!"

"You Americans are so backward," she said, smiling at him. "My turn now."

Matthew took a healthy swig from his glass, and they kissed. He pushed the wine and then his tongue into her mouth.

"Mmm," she said, after she'd swallowed. "Well done."

"I want to do that again."

They repeated the exchange. Matthew was experiencing a joy that transcended anything he'd felt for a long time. Joy for him had become a rare oasis that appeared briefly then suddenly vanished, leaving him in the desert of his depression for weeks and months at a time.

He pulled back onto the road, and they continued their drive. As they entered the Charlevoix region, the road passed up and down increasingly steep hills; at one point they were looking down on a church spire as if they were flying in. To the right was the glistening St. Lawrence, with a freighter in the middle. Shortly afterward, they descended into Malbae and followed the signs to Le Manoir Richelieu. As it came into view, Matthew was flabbergasted at its magnificence, even though he's seen pictures of it in guidebooks. He pulled up in front of the main entrance, and a valet came around to park the car. There were several doormen, valets, and guests near the entrance, and they all gawked at Claire as she stepped out of the immaculate Jaguar. Matthew was proud of his date and glad that he had a car that matched her beauty. He felt very self-conscious as he got out and handed the keys to the valet. They entered the lobby to check in. Matthew had one small bag with him; Claire had nothing but her purse. They took the elevator to the third floor, and found their room. Once inside, Matthew turned, drew her close, and kissed her deeply. His hands were on her hips, and the curve of her body electrified him, especially as he knew he would posses her later that night.

"Shall we go for a drink?" he asked at last.

"Sounds good to me."

They went down to the first floor, and followed the wall signs to the lounge. There were only a few guests there. The bartender came over and said something in French.

"Parlez-vous anglais?" Matthew asked.

The waiter shook his head. "Non," he said.

Matthew looked at Claire for help.

"What would you like?" she asked.

"I don't know, some kind of ale, perhaps?"

She glanced at the taps. "Deux blondes," she said.

"What's that?"

"They're light ales," she said. "IPAs".

"Oh, great."

The bartender brought their ales, filled to the brims, and Matthew paid him. They took their drinks out onto the terrace, which overlooked the gardens below and the St. Lawrence further on.

Matthew shook his head. "This is incredible," he said. "I feel like I'm at a chateaux in France."

"Yes, it is nice," she replied.

Matthew turned to her. "I'm so glad that you're with me, Claire. The journey would have been empty without you. You've made this a very special day for me."

She smiled. "The day is still young."

"Geez, I can't imagine it being any better."

"You Americans have such stunted imaginations."

He laughed. "Vive la Quebec libre!"

She laughed. "Your heart is in the right place." They both stood admiring the view for a while, sipping their ales.

When they'd finished, Matthew asked, "How about a nice dinner in the hotel restaurant?"

"That sounds nice."

"Great. Why don't we go in, and I'll make reservations."

"Okay, you do that," she said. "I'm going to do a bit of clothes shopping in the hotel boutiques, and I'll meet you back at the room in half an hour."

Matthew felt another thrill pass through him. "Okay. See you in half an hour."

He went up to the room and pulled out some nicer clothes from his bag. He put on his nice khakis, a pink button-down Oxford shirt, and the blue blazer he'd brought, even though it had some wrinkles.

A short while later, Claire came into the room. Matthew almost gasped. She was wearing a short royal blue sweater dress which hugged every curve on her body, and black silk stockings.

"Oh my god," he said. "You look incredible."

"I know," she said, smiling.

"Can I just rape you right now?"

"No, you may not."

"Oh, so you're going to torture me all night having a dinner and all that?"

"Yes. That's exactly what I intend to do."

Matthew smiled. "Well, I don't want to waste another minute. Let's get some dinner."

He kissed her, then placed his hand on her lower back as they exited the room. The contact sent another charge through his body.

They entered the dining room, and as a waiter led them to their table, every male stole a glance at her, if not a swivel-headed stare. He was reminded of his dinner with Maria. But Claire was in a league of her own. She was truly breathtaking. He was amazed at his good fortune. The waiter pulled out the chair for her and as they were seated, Matthew found himself wondering again why this gorgeous woman had gotten into a car with a complete stranger, and was obviously going to give herself to him later that night. He was puzzled, but he didn't let it interfere with his appreciation of the moment. He was genuinely happy.

He ordered a bottle of red wine with his painfully broken French, then laughed when Claire teased him about his having ordered a pitcher of lemonade.

The wine came, and it was wonderful, as even Claire admitted. He raised his glass and said, "To random encounters on rue St. Jean." She touched glasses with him and drank.

As he read through the menu, he decided he would go French Quebecois all the way. He ordered escargots as an appetizer, and tortiere, the meat pie, as his main course. Claire ordered a chicken caeser salad.

As they sipped their wine, Matthew watched her as she was looking out the window toward the river. For a few moments he saw it again: a look of deep sadness. He almost said something, almost asked her what was wrong, but he decided not to. It wasn't his business, and he didn't want to do anything that might upset her. When their dinners arrived, the pleased look on her face made him glad that he hadn't said anything.

They enjoyed a marvelous dinner as darkness fell and the candlelit dining room grew more romantic by the minute. As they were enjoying desert and cognac after dinner, Matthew felt the side of her ankle rubbing up and down against the inside of his leg, and excitement surged through his body. By now they were both tipsy, if not drunk, between all the wine and the cognac, but it did nothing to blunt his desire; in fact, it seemed to be fueling it. As he felt her leg against his, he stared into her beautiful eyes, and she held his gaze. Then a slight smile appeared on her glossy pink lips, and he felt something like the sensation he'd had in a singular dream all his life, where he runs to the top of a perfectly green, grassy hill, and with outstretched arms leaps into the air and glides on a gentle breeze, circling around and swooping as freely as an eagle.

He paid the bill, and kept his arm around the curve of her waist as they left the dining room and returned to their room. Neither of them said a word until they'd closed the door. Then there was an explosion of mutual desire as they kissed frenetically and simultaneously tore at each other's clothes, their breathing growing faster and deeper, till they were in a kind of breathless, uncontrolled frenzy. Matthew backed her against the door, then wrapped his arms around her thighs and lifted her so that he could thrust up into the naked vortex of her sex. "Oui! Oui!" she cried out, and the very sound of her ecstasy drove him even higher into his own passion, and as she continued to cry out, he felt himself releasing inside her again and again and again, and the wave of bliss engulfed him so powerfully that he feared he'd lose consciousness and drop her. He lowered her roughly, and fell onto the bed, absolutely breathless.

She followed and collapsed beside him, panting just as hard. "Oh my god," she said.

Matthew panted a few more times, his heart pounding, and echoed her words: "Oh my god."

They rolled and held each other for a long while without speaking, and Matthew felt the beating, or pounding, really, of her heart, even through the pounding of his own. In time he felt her hand stroking his body, his sex, and as he became aroused again, he did the same to her. Soon he entered her again, only this time their love-making was very slow, gentle, sensuous. She took him in her mouth, and in turn he tasted of her sex. Once again their breathing became short and desperate, and as he felt her coming again, writhing beneath him, he again thrust as deep as he could inside her and stayed there, letting the rhythmic gyrations of her hips do the rest, until again the universe collapsed into the sensations that were rolling through him, and he groaned and again released himself endlessly into the depths of her body. The experience was incredible for Matthew; he had never received such pleasure from a woman's body before. There was something magical about it, and he did everything he could to repay her in kind for what she was doing to him.

They made love for hours, until finally, in what must have been the early hours of the morning, he rolled onto his back, and whispered, "Claire, c'est finis."

She drew close to him, her head resting on his chest, her hand gently sliding over his stomach, his chest, his cheek. Then they both lay still for a while, their hearts pounding but gradually slowing down. Just as Matthew was about to sink into sweet oblivion, he felt Claire's upper body begin to shudder and he thought he heard the slightest sound of weeping. He was instantly alert, and he listened intently. He felt her trying to suppress any sound or movement, but he heard it and felt it nonetheless. Then he felt the warmth of her tears on his chest. He was alarmed and confused. He didn't know what to do, so he simply drew her closer, and brought his right arm over her waist, and squeezed her close. After a few minutes she seemed to calm, and then, after a few more minutes, her body was still and he heard the slow, slight breathing that signified sleep. He relaxed, and without thought, sank into sleep himself.

When he woke in the morning, around eight o'clock, Claire was not there. For a moment, he thought she might be in the bathroom, but when he got up to look, she wasn't there either. Yet he saw her jeans and blouse on the chair. He figured she had gone down to the café near the lobby to get some coffee. He was still naked, and his nakedness reminded him of the passionate night they had had. He felt the stirrings of arousal. He went to the windows, which overlooked the St. Lawrence and the hotel terraces and gardens below. He was puzzled to see several policemen down on the lowest terrace, the one that rimmed the edge of the bluff leading down to the river. He felt a twinge in his gut.

He dressed quickly, in a kind of automatic state, and went down and out of the hotel as fast as he could. He went down to the lowest terrace, and went over to one of the policemen.

"Excusez-moi. Parlez-vous anglais?"

"Yes, a bit," the officer replied in a thick accent.

"What's going on here?" Matthew asked, with a rising sense of dread.

The officer eyed him for a moment. "A woman's body was discovered on the rocks below, at the edge of the river."

Matthew felt like he might be sick. "Oh, god," he said.

A look of intense interest appeared on the officer's face. "Is there something you can tell me?"

"What does she look like?" he asked, trying to suppress his panic.

"A blond woman, mid-thirties perhaps, in a blue dress."

Matthew felt as if he'd been punched in the stomach. "Oh, my god," he said, and he raised his hands to cover his face. He feared he might vomit.

"Did you know her?" the officer asked. "Can you tell me anything?"

Matthew lowered his hands. "I picked up a woman in Quebec City yesterday, a stranger, and we spent the day . . . and night together. When I woke up this morning she was gone. She was an attractive blond in her thirties, and had been wearing a blue, a royal blue, dress. Her name was Claire. I don't know her last name."

"So, you last saw her last night?"

"Yes . . . into the early morning hours, when we were in bed."

"Her body was just brought up. Can you identify her?"

Matthew nodded his head. He couldn't speak.

The officer led him over to an ambulance. The rear doors were open. He stepped into the back, along with the officer. The officer pulled back a sheet.

Matthew looked upon Claire's broken face, and burst into tears. "That's her," he gasped.

The officer pulled the sheet back over her face, and got out of the ambulance.

The rest of the morning was a blur for Matthew. He led several officers up to his room, and showed them the clothes she'd left, and also her purse, which was lying out of site on a chair drawn up to the desk. He wondered if they considered him a suspect, and if they would detain him for questioning. They asked him lots of questions, and he answered them as truthfully as he could. The only meaningful things he thought he could tell them was that she had allowed herself to be picked up by a total stranger, and that that after they'd made love, late at night, she had wept in his arms. That was it. He gave the officers a complete, formal statement, and after they'd taken information from his passport, they told him that he could go, but asked that he make himself available should they need to contact him for further questioning. He readily agreed.

He quickly gathered his belongings, had his car brought up, and left as fast as he could. He felt like throwing up.

As he drove south along the river towards Quebec City, his sorrow about Claire became clouded by self-recriminations. Had he said or done something which triggered some overwhelmingly painful memory for her? He wracked his brain, but could think of nothing, and did not remember seeing any kind of reaction from her which would hint at it, except for those few moments of tears which had puzzled him. The whole day and night had seemed like a beautiful experience for both of them, from the car ride till they went to sleep after a night of wonderful and passionate sex. But he remembered those tears. And he remembered how he'd been struck by something sad about her, in her eyes, when he first saw her at the café. And during dinner, later on, he saw it again. He wished he had probed a bit, said something about her looking sad, and did she want to talk. Perhaps if he'd done so, she would have opened up, and perhaps he could have shared some of his own history, and had a frank discussion about depression and suicide. Perhaps if he had, she'd still be alive. But he'd not wanted to pry, and perhaps spoil what had been up till then a wonderful day. But he regretted not asking, and it saddened him deeply. The tears began to flow.

As he approached Quebec City he decided he was too emotionally distraught, and physically worn out, to continue all the way back to Boston. He decided to check back into the hotel he'd stayed at, and try to rest and recover. Maybe he'd even stay a few more days. This cheered him a bit, because he loved Quebec City more than any place he'd ever been, and he cherished whatever time he spent there. It would be good for him; certainly better than returning to his depressing little room back in Boston. Yes, he'd return to his beloved Quebec City.

In Place Royal late that afternoon, he sat down on the terrace of a cafe, and ordered a double espresso. He lit a cigarette and sat looking out over the cobbled square. A bust of Louis XIV, a gift from the French government long ago, faced him from atop a marble column ten yards away. A few small groups of tourists, mostly Japanese, filtered in an out of the square. The sun was declining and long sharp shadows fell across Place Royal. He studied the modest, stone, seventeenth century church, Notre Dame des Victoires, for a long while, and finally decided to pay it a visit. He settled his bill and walked across the cobblestones and up the few stone stairs to the entrance. He told himself that he wanted to inspect the beauty of the church's interior, but he knew, or rather felt, that there was more to it. That he wanted something else. In the silent dimness of the nave, he walked up the center aisle, and sat in one of the pews near the front. There were only a few tourists, and they were in the outer aisles, admiring the plaques and ornamentation on the walls. He sat for a long while staring at the baroque artistry of the apse, the stained glass, the carvings, the candles, the altar. He felt a sense of peace. The urge to kneel came over him, and he moved forward from his seat and knelt on the cushioned bar. He placed his elbows on the top of the pew in front of him, and without thinking, clasped his hands together. He realized he was in the classic posture to pray, and felt self-conscious. He felt an urge to say something, but nothing came to his mind. But he continued to kneel there, hands clasped, staring at the large gold cross on the altar. Finally he thought of Claire, and he was overcome with sadness. And then words came to his lips. He whispered them:

"Dear Lord, I don't know if you even exist, but if you do, please take care of Claire, give her peace and happiness for all eternity."

Then he thought of the little English boy. "And Lord, the little boy who was murdered in England, please, God, please take care of him forever. Let him be a happy child, with no memory of his death, and give him the happiness that he surely deserves forever and ever."

He sat for a moment, his mind empty of thought. Then he recited the Lord's Prayer:

> *Our Father, who art in heaven, hallowed be thy name; thy kingdom come, thy will be done, on Earth as it is in Heaven. give us this day our daily bread; and forgive us our trespasses, as we forgive those who trespass against us; and lead us not into temptation, but deliver us from evil.*
> *Amen.*

When finished, he sat back in the pew, and realized he was trembling. He sat there for a long while, almost void of thought. Then he left the pew and went to the bank of candles flickering in the front corner of the church. He place a few dollars in the collection box, then lit a candle for Claire, another for the English boy, and then, after a hesitation, one for his father. His heart was full and he felt a strange emotion he couldn't identify. He looked up at the marble statue of Christ, and then across at the tender-looking statue of Mary. He lowered his eyes, and felt them welling with tears. He turned and walked out of the church. He wasn't sure what had happened in there, but knew it was a lot more profound than just admiring ecclesiastical art and architecture. He felt a kind of calm, almost peace, enveloping him. He felt, in some way, like a person different from the one who'd walked into the church half an hour ago.

As darkness fell over Quebec City, he wandered the streets with no destination, taking in the beauty of the narrow streets, the colorful cafes and shops all warmly lit. He felt a connection with the city; everything seemed softened into a blur of sight and sound. He smiled at pretty girls, visited bookshops, stopped for an ale at a pub, and continued walking about until it was late in the evening. He finally returned to his room and fully clothed, laid down on the bed. He wasn't tired, and laid there staring at the ceiling. He was aware that he was in some sort of strange mental and emotional state, but didn't want to ruin it by analyzing it. He just laid there, without moving, for hours. He decided that when he got home he would visit a priest at St. Mary's, the Catholic church down the street from his apartment, and talk to him. He drifted off into a dreamless sleep.

When he awoke, it was mid-morning, and he felt rested. However, the sort of mystical state he'd been in the previous evening was gone, and the thought of Claire quickly weighed on him. He became sad and depressed. He went out to get some breakfast, and with some hesitation, decided to go to the boulangerie where he'd first seen Claire. He didn't go there strictly because of that memory, but also because he loved the place. But as he walked in, and looked at the empty table where she had been sitting, he felt a pounding wave of sadness. He ordered a coffee and a croissant, and sat down on the same stool at her table. The sadness was palpable, and he wondered why he was doing this, why he was willfully sticking a knife in himself. He thought about leaving, but somehow, that thought made him feel like he would be turning his back on her, and he didn't want to do that. He wanted to think about her. Not her death, but about their time together, and who she was, at least as much as he had been learn in their few hours together. As he sat there thinking, he remembered how as they'd been driving to Charlevoix, they'd passed within site of a large church, a basilica or cathedral of some sort, and that Claire had said it was a site of pilgrimage for people from around the world looking for consolation and even healing. The more he thought about it, the more he wanted to go there. He took out his pocket guide to Quebec, and studied the map of the region northeast of Quebec City, along the St. Lawrence. Sure enough, he saw something identified as the Shrine of St. Anne de Beaupre, about twenty miles away. He decided twenty miles by car was a pilgrimage easily made. He left the café, and with a last look through the window where he first saw Claire, he walked down rue St. Jean to the garage where his car was parked.

As he drove north and east out of the city, he couldn't help but think of making this same drive with Claire. As he passed the bridge that led to the Ile d'Orlean, where they'd visited the vineyard, he looked at the empty seat next to him and felt sick to his stomach. He started to cry. He wanted so badly to know what had driven her to do what she'd done, and yet, he already knew. That's what tore at him more than anything. He wished that somehow they'd talked about suicide, that he'd been able to share his experiences and learn what was tearing her apart.

He kept on driving, and following the signs, soon turned off the highway onto a smaller, two lane road that led to the village of Beaupre. Suddenly, looming in the distance above the modest little homes and shops of the village, he saw the huge, magnificent twin spires of the shrine. It was a breathtaking sight. It reminded him of the great cathedrals in France and England he'd often studied in books. As he approached he was impressed even more by its size and grandeur. He pulled into a nearby parking lot, and walked to the handsome plaza before the shrine. He stopped and gazed up at the huge façade and the spires that rose up into the sky. He was struck by how bright and clean the stonework was, completely free of any dirt or soot that generally coats even the most modest churches or public buildings, or any buildings, really. It was if it had been scrubbed clean that morning. Perhaps because it was a weekday, there were relatively people milling around, though there were a few tour buses parked on the road nearby. He walked through the huge doors, which were open, and his eyes adjusted to the semi-dim interior. It was a stunning sight. As he walked up the center aisle, it dawned on him that he wasn't here as a tourist. He was here for some reason that wasn't clear to him, but he knew it wasn't just to look at stained glass windows, as magnificent as they were. He walked about halfway up the aisle, and moved into one of the pews. There were missals lying on the pews, and he picked one up. The text was in both French and English. He flipped through it, and came across a prayer which struck him. He sat there, and read it and read it again. He started to weep. And once the gates had opened, he couldn't control the flood. He bent forward, his elbows on his knees and his face in his hands, and cried and sobbed. He was conscious of his breakdown, aware that people might be looking at him, but he didn't care. He let it come out. When he finally stopped crying, he didn't change his position. He sat there with his face in his hands, his mind falling into a kind of blank, empty, state. He was reminded of his visit to Notre Dame des Victoires in Place Royal the day before. What, he wondered, was going on? Once again, he thought that he needed to visit a priest when he got back home. He remembered his meeting with Jonathan, his Congregational minister, and shuddered. He feared that he'd get the same empty pablum. In fact, the more he thought about it, the more he thought that meeting with a priest would snuff whatever small, flickering flame of spirituality was glowing inside him. As he thought again about his meeting with Jonathan, he felt something cold pass through him and he stood up. He wanted to leave. He walked down the aisle in a state of confusion, and winced as he exited into the bright sunshine. He walked to his car without looking back, but just before he got in, he looked up at the spires, and at the moment the great bells of the shrine began tolling and again he felt something warm stir inside him. He stood beside his car, listening to the bells till they'd ceased ringing. Then he got into his car and sat for a moment before starting the engine. He was glad that he'd come here.

He had his sun-roof open on the drive back to Quebec City, and the rushing sound of the wind blew away all his thoughts, which was a welcome relief. He spent the rest of the day as he had the day before, wandering the narrow, colorful streets of the Old Town, within the city gates. He went to bed early that night, and consequently woke very early. By six a.m. he was out the door, headed for Paillard's once again, on foot. As he turned the corner onto rue St. Jean, he saw a bouquet of flowers scattered across the street, as if tossed from a car window. The sight saddened him. He wondered what story lay behind those flowers; had two would-be lovers had an argument in the car, leading the girl in her bitterness to throw away the flowers he had given her?

He picked up a yellow rose that had not been crushed by the traffic and brought it with him to Paillard's. He ordered a croissant and coffee, and once again sat at the high table where he'd first seen Claire. When he finished his breakfast, he stood and, thinking of Claire, placed the rose across the top of the table. His eyes welled up. He decided he would leave for Boston this morning, but decided to take a last walk about town before he left. He headed up towards the Chateau Frontenac, and the jardin des Gouverneurs just beyond. He turned right, and climbed the hill to the Parc de Moulin de Cavalier, his favorite park in the city. It was high atop a rampart, and it overlooked a sea of colorful rooftops, church spires, and distant mountains. He felt that something had changed in him during this trip to Quebec. Despite his stirring experiences in some of the churches, he knew that he hadn't suddenly gained a faith in God, let alone in Jesus Christ and everything that entailed. He only knew that there had been some sort of tectonic shift, a cry for something, and that he had a strong desire to talk to a priest when he got back. He heard the majestic bells of the Cathedral of Notre Dame toll seven times.

After he'd checked out and retrieved his car from the garage under City Hall, he found his way to St. Louis Gate and with the same sadness he always felt when he left this city, he headed west then south over the St. Lawrence River. He was on his way. He drove with all the windows and the sunroof open;

once again the noisy blast of wind rushing through the car served as a kind of anesthetic, pushing away his thoughts and allowing him to slip into a kind of alert trance, where only the road, the wind and the passing scenery held his attention. In a way, he hoped he'd never reach Boston; that he could go on and on in this vacuous state.

Chapter Seven

He arrived at his apartment in mid afternoon and found the place even more depressing than he'd feared. He had a momentary thought of going back to Quebec City; he could be back there by midnight. But he also knew that he'd only be running away, and that going back to Quebec would only postpone the grim feelings he had now.

He unpacked his bags, then made the call. A woman, probably a nun, answered the phone. He explained that he was in trouble, emotionally, and wished to make an appointment to speak in private to one of the priests.

"Would you like to come over now? Several of the priests are here, and I'm sure one of them would be happy to talk to you."

He was taken aback a bit; he hadn't expected an immediate invitation, and didn't feel ready to talk to a priest that evening. "Umm, I can't come over this evening, but could I make an appointment for tomorrow morning or afternoon?"

"Can I put you on hold for a moment?"

A moment later she came back on line. "Father Hanlon would be happy to see you at ten a.m. Is that okay?"

"Yes," he said. "That would be great."

"Okay," she said. "Just ring at the rectory, and someone will show you in till Father Hanlon comes in. He might be a few minutes late, but he'll be there."

He thanked her and hung up. He was filled with a mix of excitement and fear. He tried to downplay it; to tell himself that he should expect nothing, if not worse, and not let himself be crushed again with anger and disappointment.

He slept fitfully that night, and got up at five a.m. He didn't know what to do with himself till his appointment at ten. Finally he dug out his Bible from the stacks of books piled on the floor, and turned to the book of Job. He identified with him: getting shit on by God, or Life, or something. Or perhaps it was the great Nothing, the dark emptiness void of any justice, meaning or sense; the absence of anything but a sort of blind malevolence, as if he were caught in an avalanche of snow or rock. He was struck by these words of Job:

Therefore I will not restrain my mouth; I will speak in the anguish of my spirit; I will complain in the bitterness of my soul.

    Shortly before ten he walked over to the rectory and rang the bell. He felt a knot in his stomach. A middle aged nun answered the door, showed him into a parlor, and told him that Father Hanlon would be with him shortly. He sat down in an easy chair, and looked around the room. It was decorated simply, and he saw some of the things he'd expected to see: a wooden crucifix on the wall, a blue and white porcelain of Mary on a shelf, a portrait of what was probably St. Agnes, and a black leather Bible on the coffee table, along with some Catholic magazines and brochures. He noted the box of tissues as well. No doubt a lot of tears had been shed in this room. He hoped he wouldn't have to use them. He wanted to keep his cool. He wanted to be open, frank and sincere with the priest, but he decided he wasn't going to take any bullshit from him. He would respect the collar, but if the priest started spouting the same platitudes as his former minister, Jonathan, he'd get up and leave. In fact, the very memory of his meeting with Jonathan riled him and put him in a skeptical mood. He tried to contain this by telling himself that he needed to keep an open mind, but he couldn't help it: if there was a god, he was mightily pissed off at him, and if there wasn't a god, then he was just plain pissed off. It was beginning to feel like a no-win situation. He was tempted to get up and leave, but he decided to at least extend the courtesy of meeting with the priest, since it was he himself who had requested the meeting.

    When Father Hanlon entered the room, Matthew rose to shake his hand. "Hi, Father, I'm Matthew. Thanks for seeing me." The priest was a slender, dark-haired man about his own age, which surprised Matthew a bit because for some reason he'd expected a wizened, older priest.

    The priest smiled warmly and said he was happy to see him, and motioned for him to sit down. The priest sat in a chair close to, and at an angle to, Matthew's.

    "How can I help?" the priest asked.

    Matthew was silent for a moment. He lowered his eyes to the priest's collar, the sharp contrast of black and white, then looked him in the eyes. "I don't know how or if you can help me, Father, but I do need help. I'm drowning."

    "Sister Margaret told me that you are suffering from some sort of emotional crisis."

    "Yes, I am. Actually, I guess it could be called a spiritual crisis as well, but perhaps they are one and the same. I don't know."

The priest leaned forward in his chair, his hands clasped. "Tell me, as best you can, what's troubling you."

"Well, it started last year." He paused for a moment, and sighed deeply. "Do you remember a murder in England last year, where a four year old boy was lured from his mother at a mall by two older boys, and they took him across town and threw rocks at him and kicked him and left him on a railroad track, to be cut in half?"

The priest nodded and frowned. "Yes, I do remember it. That was horrible."

"Yeah, well, when I first read about it, it broke me up so bad that I became virtually dysfunctional. It was like a huge crack in my foundation. I couldn't get him out of my mind, and I shed so many tears for him, day after day. The thing is, I didn't, and don't, really know why. I mean, the papers are full of terrible tragedies every day, and while they're troubling, they don't make me go off the deep end like that. I mean, thousands of children die every day from starvation. That saddens me, but it doesn't make me break down in tears every day. But that murder devastated me. I couldn't understand why I was reacting that way, and I couldn't understand how God could let that innocent little boy suffer and die the way he did. And his poor mother . . ." he paused. "She's going to suffer and blame herself for the rest of her life. I just don't understand it, Father. I was so bitter and angry at a god who is supposedly so merciful and loving, that I decided that he's either a god not worth worshipping, or that he doesn't exist at all. And I'm leaning towards the latter. I just can't reconcile that murder with a god who cares. I mean, God is supposed to be providential, right? So, if he can intercede in our lives whenever he wants, why didn't he intercede on behalf of that little boy? How can God just pick and choose those he's going to help, and those he's going to ignore? Or, like I said, maybe he doesn't even exist, which would explain why so many terrible things happen in this world."

The priest was silent for a long moment. He looked into Matthew's eyes and said, "Matthew, I'm not sure that I can answer that question for you . . . or answer it in a way that will make you feel any better about it."

Matthew was startled by the priest's words. Yet after he got over the initial surprise, he realized that he'd gained an instant respect for the priest because he didn't pretend to have the answers. In fact, the priest had given the only answer that Matthew could accept. Matthew didn't say anything, but just sat looking at the priest.

The priest continued. "But I can tell you this, Matthew. As much as I believe in God—and my faith is very strong—he is also a mystery to me. In fact, I believe there's only man who has ever, and can ever, truly understand God, and that's his son, Jesus Christ. I think anyone else who claims to understand God's ways is either speculating or deluded. Or both."

Matthew nodded again, but still said nothing.

The priest continued. "My own mother was killed three years ago in a totally bizarre accident. She was coming home from work, and was crushed by a falling church steeple."

Matthew's jaw dropped. "A church steeple?"

"A church steeple, of all things. There were heavy winds that day, and the steeple on an old, colonial church toppled and landed on my mother's car just as she was driving by. She was killed instantly. Just like that, she was gone. And I couldn't understand it. I couldn't even accept it at first. I mean, killed by a falling church steeple? It was just so random, and even obscene. If she'd left work a minute later, she'd be alive. It was a terrible time for me."

Matthew lowered his eyes. "Jesus, Father, I'm so sorry for your loss."

"Thank you," the priest said.

Matthew was silent for a moment. Then he said, "My father committed suicide when I was seven years old. I was the one who found him hanging in the basement."

The priest hung his head for a moment, then looked up at Matthew. "I can't even imagine what that must have been like for you."

"Yeah. I'm not sure I've ever gotten over it."

They were both silent for a long moment. "Let me ask you this," the priest said, at last. "You said a moment ago that you are leaning towards disbelief in God. I take it that means you are open to the possibility that he exists?"

"Yes, I suppose," Matthew replied. "But like I said, if he does exist I don't think he deserves to be worshipped. I mean, there's a part of me that sort of wants to believe in a loving god, and wanting to believe actually feels good and makes me wonder what it would be like if I really and truly did believe, with all my heart, and that perhaps it would save me. But at the same time, my mind won't let me truly believe. I feel like a kid who finally discovers there is no Santa Claus. Once he realizes that, he can't go back. He might still want to believe that Santa exists, but no matter how much he wishes it, he knows the truth."

"But you're not quite in that situation, are you? The truth hasn't been revealed to you. God is still a possibility for you, based on what you just said."

Matthew nodded. "Okay."

The priest was silent for a moment. "You expressed a desire to be saved," he said at last. "What do you feel you need to be saved from?"

"From death, Father. I mean that literally. From killing myself."

A look of concern passed over the priest's face. "I see," he said. "Have you sought psychiatric counseling?"

"I've been down that road all too often. My diagnosis is clinical depression, with psychotic episodes. I've attempted suicide in the past, and have undergone hospitalizations, and therapy and shock treatments, and been on all kinds of medications. And nothing has helped, or at least, not for long." He paused for a moment. "I'm just very tired, Father. I'm just so tired of it all. And a part of me, a big part of me, wants to quit, to die. But a part of me wants to live, too. I guess that's why I'm here."

"Well, I'm glad you're here," the priest said. "I must tell you, though, that faith in God and Church is not likely to cure you of clinical depression. It's possible, I mean God has certainly worked greater miracles. But here's the important thing, Matthew. Turning to God, having faith and hope, can give you the strength to go on despite your illness, to cope with the worst things and to go on living. God's love is a lifeline offered to all who will accept it. It's there for you, if you're willing to take it."

Matthew nodded, but didn't say anything. He was thinking hard about what the priest was saying.

After a moment, the priest asked, "Have you ever believed?"

"Yes, I guess I did at one time, but it was kind of a passive thing. I don't think I was spiritually invested very much, or gave it much thought, really. God was just this thing I prayed to occasionally, usually for stupid things like letting the Sox win the World Series, and church was just this place I went to on Sundays to sing hymns, recite creeds I only half-believed, and go to coffee hour afterwards with all the other well-to-do suburbanites and eat blueberry cake. It was just this thing I did every week, without giving it much thought."

"Are you a Catholic?"

"Well, I was raised as a Catholic, if that's what you mean, but in my twenties I sort of fell away from the Church and, more from convenience than anything else, joined my wife's Congregational Church, the U.C.C."

The priest gave a hint of a smile. "I hate to break this to you, Matthew, but in the eyes of the Church you are still a Catholic, despite your rejection of her and your anger and doubt about God."

"Well, what's the point of that?" Matthew said, a bit of exasperation in his voice.

The priest was silent for a moment. "Are you familiar with the parable of the Prodigal Son?"

"Yes, of course."

"Okay, think of it this way. You are the prodigal son, and God, through the Catholic Church, is your father. You may have run away, and squandered everything, and fallen into misery, and cursed everyone and everything, but you are still your father's son, and he has never stopped loving you. And when you finally, in desperation, go back to your father, he welcomes you with open arms and showers you with love. You have returned, and you are nourished by your father's love and forgiveness. You are saved, and joy returns to you under your father's roof."

"Okay, good answer," Matthew said. "I guess I can accept that."

"Do you like to read?" the priest asked.

Matthew nodded. "Yes, I do. Very much."

"Well, I have a book that I think might interest you, called *The Return of the Prodigal Son*, by a priest named Henri Nouwen. He saw Rembrandt's painting depicting the son's reunion with his father, and Nouwen was so taken with the painting that he wrote a book about it. But it's not really about the painting. He uses the painting as a means of understanding the true meaning of the parable. Would you be interested in reading it?"

Matthew nodded. "Yes, I would."

Father Hanlon smiled. "Okay, good. And there's another book I think you'd be interested in. Have you read Lee Strobel's *The Case for Christ*?"

"No. Never heard of it."

"I think you might really like that book. Strobel is a highly educated, hard-nosed legal reporter in Chicago, and was an atheist who decided to meet with the most prominent Biblical scholars, and even archaeologists and psychologists, around the country, and ask them pointed and direct questions about the story of Christ. In effect, he played Devil's advocate, and his penchant for getting at the facts in talking with these authorities is striking. It's a remarkable story; a journey, really, which led to his acceptance of Christ. I think it will directly address some of your own questions and doubts."

"That sounds like something right up my alley. I'd like to read it."

"If I lend you these books, will you promise to read them and come back to me so we can talk about them?"

"Yes. I'll do that, Father. I can make that promise."

"Wonderful," he replied, and stood up. "I'll be right back." He took a few steps then turn around. "By the way," he said. "Do you like classical music?"

"As a matter of fact I do," Matthew replied. "I'm not real knowledgeable about it, but I do enjoy it."

"Good," the priest said, and he left the room.

Matthew sat and tried to absorb the conversation. He felt something like hope, and was anxious to read the books the priest had recommended. He marveled at how different this meeting was—with a priest he'd never met—from his meeting with his long-time minister, Jonathan, which had filled him with rage and disgust. He was glad he'd come to talk with Father Hanlon.

A few minutes later the priest returned with two books and a CD, and handed them to Matthew.

Matthew looked at the books. "Thank you, Father. I promise to read them, and come back to talk with you about them." He glanced at the CD. It was Bach's *St. Matthew Passion*. He looked at the priest.

"Are you familiar with that?" Father Hanlon asked.

"No. I don't think I've ever heard it."

"I want you to listen to it," the priest said. "It's a magnificent work, and very moving. The lyrics have been translated into English. Just listening to it is almost a religious experience. And the overture . . . well, I consider the overture to be one of the greatest pieces of music ever created."

Matthew looked at it again. The cover art showed a Renaissance painting of Christ on the cross. He looked up at the crucifix on the wall. Then he stood up. "Thank you so much for meeting with me, Father."

"Any time," the priest said. "I mean that. If you feel the need to talk before you've finished the books, please call me, or stop by."

Matthew nodded. "I will."

"And one more thing," the priest said. "I want you to promise me that if you feel the urge to harm yourself, that you'll call me, or your psychiatrist, or take yourself to the hospital. Can you promise me that?"

"Yes, I promise you."

The priest extended his hand. "Shake on it."

Matthew shook his hand.

"Okay. You've given me your word," the priest said. "You wouldn't lie to a priest, would you?"

Matthew shook his head. "No. I wouldn't."

"All right, then. I'll see you when you've finished the books. Or sooner, if you would like to talk."

Father Hanlon escorted Matthew to the door.

"Thank you again, Father. I'll see you soon."

"I look forward to it, Matthew."

Matthew opened the door and stepped out into the sunshine. As he walked home with the books under his arms, he felt a certain lightness in his stride and in his heart. He was eager to get home and start reading.

He started with *The Return of the Prodigal Son*, and stayed up all night reading it. The book, and Rembrandt's masterpiece by that name, both struck him deeply. It was a short book, and he couldn't put it down. He wept several times—sometimes because of the story, and sometimes at the memory of his own dead father. He finished it around four in the morning and went to bed exhausted, but also feeling something like joy. He felt like he was in darkness, but that he was on some sort of track that might lead him to the light. He wasn't sure what that light might be, but he was willing to walk on the track. After all, he'd done that before.

When he woke a few hours later he put the Bach into his CD player, and with his headphones on, laid back and listened. The overture did indeed sweep him away; it was like nothing he'd ever heard. And then he listened to the words of Jesus, taken from the Gospels, before his crucifixion, and somehow the beauty of the voice and the accompanying choir and strings, kept him from feeling his usual pangs of doubt or anger. Bach's faith spoke so strongly through the music that Matthew felt the music in his heart. His eyes welled several time. He marveled at the power of this music, and understood why Father Hanlon had asked him to listen to it.

When it was over, he picked up the Strobel book and started reading. And he kept on reading all day and into the night. Strobel's words, his objectivity and doubts, spoke to him. Yet Matthew's skepticism was like an opaque glass that constantly blurred what he was reading, constantly kept him on the defensive. He finally went to bed again around five in the morning, and when he woke up, he started reading again. The opacity gradually melted away, and he began to identify with Strobel's journey. Matthew was impressed by the power of the propaganda that Father Hanlon had given him. He finished the book that night, and was eager to meet with the priest to discuss it.

The following morning, he phoned the rectory, gave his name, and asked if Father Hanlon was available. The priest came to the phone. "Father," Matthew said. "I've read the books you lent me. Can I meet with you?"

"Wow. That was fast. Certainly you can come by. I'm here till late this afternoon, so come on over."

"Thank you," Matthew said. He immediately gathered the books and the CD, and headed out the door. Fifteen minutes later he was at the rectory. He asked for Father Hanlon, and was shown into the parlor again to wait. A moment later the priest came in and smiled. "Man, you don't waste any time, do you?"

"I guess I'm in crisis mode, Father."

The priest's expression became serious, and he sat down. Matthew had the books and CD in his lap.

"What did you think of them?" the priest asked.

"I'm the Prodigal Son," Father. "Or, I think I want to be. I'm not sure. But I was very moved by the book, and the painting. I wept at times; sometimes because of Nouwen's words, and sometimes just by looking at the painting itself in a new light. I identified so much with the Prodigal Son. And the Strobel book, well, that blew me away. He asked all these experts the very questions I would have asked, and many I hadn't even thought of. It was amazing. I could hardly put it down. Actually, I couldn't put either one of them down."

The priest nodded. "I had a feeling you'd like them."

"And this," Matthew said, holding up the CD, "was truly incredible. I've never been so spiritually engaged by music. It was sort of like a Gothic cathedral turned into music."

"That's an interesting way to put it. I'm glad you liked it."

"I was very moved by the repeated question, the choral refrain, in the overture: 'Look! Look where?' and then that sad response, 'On our offense.' It brought tears to my eyes, not just because of 'our offense', but because . . . because of my offense."

Father Hanlon nodded, but didn't say anything.

Matthew looked down at the books and CD in his lap and stared for a long moment. Then he placed them on the coffee table. "I'd like to talk about books, other books, if we could, Father."

"Sure," he replied.

"Let me ask you: are you familiar at all with Jean-Paul Sartre?"

"Yes, as a matter of fact, I am."

Matthew was impressed. "Well, I've read a lot of his works this past year, especially *Being and Nothingness*, which has been a kind of bible for me. Have you read that book?"

"Yes, I have."

Matthew was surprised.

"Tell me why that book has become your bible," the priest asked.

"Well, as you know, he was an atheist, and he built a philosophy that follows from his atheism. And in some strange way, it comforted me. He made me see the world in a completely different way, and his analysis of consciousness, and what it means to be human, really resonated with me. He argued that there is no such thing as destiny, or God, and that this is a scary thing, because we all wish to hand off responsibility for our lives to someone else, especially God. You know, 'God is my co-pilot,' 'Jesus take the wheel,' and all that. Sartre was a breath of cold but fresh air. It was liberating. He washed away a lot of the stuff that had been cluttering my mind, and I guess you could say that existentialism became my religion. And frankly, it's grim stuff, which perfectly mirrors my own mood."

Father Hanlon was silent for a moment. "You realize, of course, that there are Christian existentialists? People like Kierkegaard, Marcel, Maritain. Have you read any of them?"

"No, I haven't. Precisely because they're Christian. Sartre said that the whole of existentialism is predicated on the notion that there is no God. His whole philosophy is built on that. It's a philosophy that fills the void left by the absence of God. The same with Heidegger."

"So you've read Heidegger, too? *Being and Time?*"

Matthew was surprised again. "Yes," he replied. "But I guess I have a problem with Heidegger because he was an unrepentant Nazi, and was arrogant as hell. I think he said somewhere that German was the only modern language that could fully encompass philosophical thought. Considering that many of the greatest philosophers in history were French or English,

I think he must have spent too much time listening to his *Deutchland Uber Alles* records. But I did find *Being and Time* enlightening. I consider it to be one of the twin pillars of existentialism, along with Sartre's *Being and Nothingness*." He paused. "But tell me, Father, why are you so familiar with such heretics?"

Father Hanlon laughed. "Know thine enemy, right? I'm not as narrow-minded as I look. I've read quite a lot of works by thinkers who are against Christianity. Russell is another one, and Richard Dawkins, who's been all over the bestseller lists. But it was Socrates who said that the un-examined life is not worth living. So I've always examined my own life, and life in general, with a critical eye. And all my casting about always leads me to the same place I started from, which is a belief in God, and Christ."

Matthew didn't say anything to this.

"Let me ask you this," the priest said. "You said that existentialism fills the void left by the absence of God. But has it really, truthfully, filled that void for you? Has it fulfilled you? Has it helped you fight your illness? Has it given you hope, and made you feel loved?"

The priest's question's cut Matthew to the quick. He thought for a long moment, then shook his head. "No, I guess it hasn't."

"I didn't think so," the priest said. "Otherwise you wouldn't be here right now, talking to me. Sartre and Heidegger are all about the power of reason, of rationality. But that's only part of our nature as humans. Aren't we more than rational automatons who act only according to the dictates of reason? Isn't a simple work of art—a painting, a poem, music—a testament to this? And isn't it this part of us, the creative, the irrational, the spiritual, if you will, that not only makes us fully human, but that demands, even cries out, for something transcendent, something greater, to nourish us?"

Matthew didn't respond for a few moments as he thought about the priest's words. Then he looked at the priest and nodded. A moment later the story of the Prodigal Son entered his thoughts. It reminded him of another story. "Tell me, Father, what do you think of the story of Abraham and Isaac? Because I think it's an absolutely horrible story, and it's the kind of thing that really pisses me off, not only about God, but about the Bible itself. I mean, on God's command, Abraham ties up his only son and is about to plunge a knife into him, simply because this petty, insecure God wants Abraham to prove his loyalty by murdering his son. What kind of God does that? I mean, think of poor Isaac, the terror and abandonment he must have felt when his own father was about to stab him. And this story is extolled as a testament to Abraham's faith. I think that's absolutely horrible. Just like the little boy in England. What kind of providential, loving God allows—or even prompts—such cruelty? I just don't understand it."

"I understand what you're saying, Matthew. But I'll go out on a limb here and say that the story of Abraham and Isaac may never have happened. In fact, it probably didn't. But it was written thousands of years ago, when children were almost a commodity. Not that their parents didn't love them, but nonetheless, they were less sacred than they are today. I mean, during the time of the Roman Empire, sickly newborns were tossed onto a dung heap.

"Jesus," Matthew said, shaking his head.

"I know. It's horrible," the priest said. "But it was a different time then. And the purpose of the story of Abraham and Isaac, regardless of whether it actually happened or not, is this idea that Abraham's faith in God was unshakable. Abraham was prepared to sacrifice anything, even his own beloved son, if that's what God desired."

"Yeah, well, I would have told him to fuck off," Matthew said, "if you'll pardon my French. I'd sooner plunge a knife into my own breast than do it to one of my own sons."

"I know, Matthew. But this story, and I believe it is just a story, was meant to make a point about the strength of a man's faith and his respect for God's will, however cruel or incomprehensible it might seem. Again, you have to remember this story was written thousands of years ago, in a different culture."

Matthew nodded, but said nothing.

There was a long silence.

"Let me ask you this," the priest said at last. "What do you think about love?"

Matthew was puzzled. "What do you mean?"

"I mean, do you take Sartre's view of it, or do you believe that it is something transcendent?"

"That's a good question." He thought for a moment. "I guess if there's anything pure and transcendent I believe in, it's love."

"So, how do you reconcile that with Sartre's rather cynical view of love, this Sartre who never married or had any children?"

Matthew was silent for a moment. "I guess I haven't."

"So you believe in the primacy of love?"

"Yes, I suppose I do. If there's anything positive at all in my life, it's my love for my children. It's the purest, most beautiful and meaningful thing in my life, my love for them.

The priest smiled. "How many children do you have?"

"Two little boys. They're the only thing in my life that keeps me going. And it kills me that I've tried to take my life, which would only have hurt them, just as my father's suicide hurt me. I can't forgive myself for doing something that would have hurt them so much."

"You haven't mentioned your wife," Father Hanlon said.

"We're separated," Matthew said, looking down at the rug. "I don't want to get into it right now. Suffice it to say that I wrecked our marriage."

There was a long silence. Finally, Matthew said, "Father, if I were to confess to you all my sins, we'd be sitting here for hours, days, maybe months. I wouldn't even know where to begin."

"Am I to gather that you are considering the sacrament of reconciliation?"

Matthew flushed. "I . . . I don't know, Father. Something's going on with me, but I'm not really sure what it is. But I loved Nouwen's book, and I identify very strongly with the Prodigal Son. Perhaps I'm trying to come back to . . . to something. I don't really know. I'm flying by the seat of my pants here."

"And that's okay. You're not alone."

"And yet I am alone, Father. It's very difficult being an atheist, or an agnostic, or whatever the hell I am. In this country, where even our money says "In God We Trust," if you're an atheist, people look at you as if you have a pitchfork and little red horns on your head. I mean, believe it or not, I've had people tell me that if I'm an atheist then I'm guilty of the worst hubris, putting man on a pedestal above God. In fact, the exact opposite is true. It's the Christians who put man on a pedestal by declaring that we are semi-divine creatures with eternal souls whom the creator of the universe watches over every day. Me, I tend to think we're just animals with a more highly evolved brain. But we're still just creatures, like rats and mosquitoes, and when we die, we die. There's none of this life after death stuff, which seems like a complete oxymoron and plain wishful thinking. I don't believe that mosquitoes go to Heaven, and I don't believe we do either. Ashes to ashes, dust to dust. So if anyone is guilty of putting man on a pedestal, it's the Christians, not me. And it ticks me off."

The priest nodded, but didn't say anything.

"Father, look at it this way. A plane crashes and one person survives. That person starts spouting off to the news cameras about his miraculous survival, that God was by his side and answered his prayers for survival on the way down. Screw that. What about the other two hundred people? Were they less worthy of God's help? How do you think the families of the victims feel about this pious asshole's claim to have been saved by the Lord? I'm sure it sickens them, and it sickens me too." Matthew was starting to tremble in anger.

A long silence fell between them. Finally the priest said, "I hear what you're saying, Matthew. I really do."

Another long silence.

"Matthew, if you came back, like the Prodigal Son, why would you come back to the Catholic Church and not one of the liberal churches, such as the Unitarian, which barely acknowledges the existence of God, let alone the divinity of Christ and the Resurrection and an afterlife. As you know, the Catholic faith asks a lot more of its faithful than do many Protestant churches. You, of all people, are aware of that, having experienced both sides of the faith. So why, if you are so skeptical, would you want to come back to the Catholic Church?"

"Well, that's a good question, Father. Frankly, I think it comes down to what church you were raised in. For all those years, continuing through college, I was a Catholic. And for better or worse, that was the faith engraved in my mind and in my heart. And really, during the years I was in my wife's Congregational church, I always felt something was missing. I know it sounds shallow, but all the Gothic and Romanesque churches, the stained glass and vaulted ceilings, the grandeur of the litany, the priests in their collars and the nuns in their habits, the two thousand years of history, all these things somehow appeal to me, and were missing from my wife's church. I mean, to me, the Catholic Church is like a hearty, beefy meal served with a complex cabernet, and the liberal Protestant churches are kind of like a salad. I realize that the kind of building you worship in is ultimately irrelevant. Yet I've seen these massive churches down South that look like huge civic convention centers, and others, even around here, that are no more than boxy little buildings with a bunch of folding chairs. There's no sense of grandeur, of beauty, of being in someplace sacred or even special. Nothing that evokes the spiritual. And yet I can understand why Protestants, such as my wife, remain in their own churches. It's because it's what they were raised in. I mean, I have no doubt that if she or I, or even you, Father, were born into the Muslim faith, we'd be trudging off to the local mosque and bowing towards Mecca."

There was another silence.

Finally the priest spoke up. "Well, Matthew, you've said a lot. Obviously I understand what you mean about the Catholic Church compared to some of the others. Personally—and keep in mind that I am a Catholic priest—I do happen to think the Catholic Church is the true church. I'd be remiss in my duties as a priest of this church if I thought or said otherwise."

"I can respect that," Matthew said.

"And I do truly hope, and I will pray, that you come back, like the Prodigal Son, to this Church. God, and this church, want to welcome you back with open arms, to forgive your transgressions, and celebrate your return with love. And I believe you will feel that, and understand that, and find peace in that."

Matthew didn't say anything.

"In a way," the priest continued, "the Prodigal Son had to die before he went home. In a similar way, Matthew, you have to die in order to live again in God's grace. Do you understand what I mean by that?"

"I'm not sure"

"Okay. What I mean is this: you need to turn around, turn your back on your present life—to die, in effect—in order to go home as the Prodigal Son did. God the father awaits you with open arms, but you must first turn around and begin the journey home."

Matthew nodded. "I understand." He sat for a while, staring at the floor. Finally he spoke up. "I have to tell you, Father, how much your words, your insights, your truly listening to me, have meant to me. I have to tell you that when I went to the minister of my U.C.C. church after the murder of the little English boy, I came out of that meeting angry at him, and angry at God. In fact, I could say that the loss of what little faith I had started with that meeting."

Father Hanlon frowned. "Why is that? What happened?"

"Well, after I'd spilled my guts, and even wept, he proceeded to spout all these scripted lines, as if I was just a variable in an equation that could be solved by reciting a few pat phrases. I just never had the feeling that he was really listening to me." Matthew shook his head. "I don't know where all this is leading me, Father, but I must tell you that I've had a very different experience with you. I feel like you are really listening to me, really trying to understand me, and are trying hard to help me. You're speaking to me in my own language. Like I said, I don't know where this is leading me, but I really and truly appreciate what you are doing. You're a credit to your profession."

"Well, thank you," the priest said. He smiled. "I'm no super-priest. I'm just trying to earn my pay, and maybe win a shot at the papacy."

Matthew smiled. "That would be cool. Then I could say I knew you when you were just a humble priest and I didn't have to kiss your ring."

Father Hanlon laughed. "Actually, I was just going to put on my college ring and ask you to kiss it. Just to get used to the feeling."

Matthew laughed too. "Where did you go to college, Father?"

"I went to The Catholic University of America."

Matthew grinned. "I went there too!" He raised his right hand, showing his class ring.

"You're kidding," the priest said.

"No, I'm not. B.A., class of '97. When did you graduate?"

"I graduated from the theological college in '95. We were both there at the same time."

"That's so funny," Matthew said. "We probably even saw each other around campus now and then."

"We probably did."

"You want to hear something silly, Father? I used to run into the basilica before a big test and pray to God to give me a good grade."

"Hey, it couldn't have hurt, right?"

"Right. Especially if I was half-drunk and hadn't studied and really needed that Godly edge. Isn't that pathetic?"

Father Hanlon laughed. "Did it work?"

"You know, maybe it did. I graduated with honors."

"Well, there you go."

Matthew shook his head.

"Do you remember," the priest said, "ever seeing a huge, handwritten outline of Aquinas's *Summa* hanging in one of the classrooms in Caldwell Hall? It was done by a seminarian in the nineteenth century."

Matthew nodded. "Yes, I do. As a matter of fact, my very first class, my freshman year, was in that room. I distinctly remember looking at that hanging on the wall and being very impressed, even though I had no idea what it meant because it was in Latin."

"Did you study Aquinas?"

"Yes, I did. I don't remember any of it, other than vague recollections of his five proofs of God's existence, but I do remember being impressed by the fact that he reasoned everything out very thoroughly, and tried to take on all the objections that might be made to his arguments. As a matter of fact, I still have the book we used that semester, a fat Modern Library paperback of his *Summa*. For some reason, I've never been able to get rid of it. It's like a souvenir of my old Catholic days or something. Just like I still have the black rosary beads I got when I was confirmed. I haven't used them since college. In fact, the last time I went to confession was at C.U., in the lower level of the basilica. So you see, Father, even if I returned to the fold, it would take me so long to confess my sins that we'd have to have cots and provisions brought into the confessional. It would be more like an exorcism."

Father Hanlon laughed.

Matthew laughed too. It felt good to laugh. He stood up, and Father Hanlon got up too.

"Are you leaving so soon?"

Matthew nodded. "I think I've said enough for now, Father. But thank you, again. Like I said, I'm not sure where I'm going with all this, but you are helping me. And I'm grateful." He paused for a moment. "Are there any other books you might suggest I read?"

"Yeah, there's one," he said, and smiled. "It's called the Bible."

Matthew smiled back. "Point taken."

"Seriously, read the Gospels. Read Job. Read the Psalms, and Ecclesiastes. There's a lot there that might speak to you."

Matthew nodded. "I've actually been doing a little reading. I read Job."

"Very good. You might want to read Aquinas, too, for the very reasons you mentioned. It might appeal to your reason and intellect."

"I might do that," Matthew said.

Father Hanlon grasped his hand. "I'll see you again soon?"

Matthew nodded. "Yes. Very soon, I hope."

"Good. I look forward to it. And please remember, you can call me any time, okay?"

"Thank you, Father." They walked to the door. Matthew smiled at the priest. "Go, Cardinals," he said.

"Go, Cardinals," the priest replied. "Oh, by the way. Do you remember the motto on the Catholic University seal? It's on your ring."

"As a matter of fact I do. I suppose you want me to say it."

Father Hanlon smiled. "Yes, I do."

"Okay. But I do this under duress. It's 'Deus Mea Lux Est.'"

"Meaning what?"

"Father, you're making this very painful."

"Too bad. Tell me what it means."

"It means, 'God is my light.'"

Father Hanlon grinned. "Okay. I just wanted to hear you say it."

Matthew faked a look of distress. "That's not fair, Father, and I reserve the right to deny having said what I just said."

Father Hanlon smiled. "Go Cardinals."

Matthew smiled and shook his head. He stepped outside, and felt the sun on his face. He walked away feeling unsettled but oddly happy. He felt a strong connection to Father Hanlon, and felt he was on the right path, even though his brain was resisting.

A few days later, while reading from the New Testament, Matthew suddenly closed it. A wave of doubt was rolling over him, and he said out loud, "What the hell am I doing?" It was nice to enjoy the warm and fuzzy feeling of sitting in an empty church, or talking to Father Hanlon, or reading books. But the bottom line is that in order to reconcile himself with the Church, he would have to believe not only in God, but in Christ as well, and believe that he was the Son of God, and that he was resurrected from the dead. He'd have to believe in an afterlife. Even if his heart wanted to believe all this, he just couldn't see himself believing. He thought again of the Santa Claus analogy: even if you want to believe in Santa, you can't believe once you've learned he doesn't exist.

But then he re-played his conversations with Father Hanlon, and a warm counter-wave rolled over him. Unlike with Santa Clause, Matthew hadn't learned as a fact that God doesn't exist. He hadn't learned as a fact that Christ wasn't the Son of God, or that he hadn't risen from the dead. He'd only formed an opinion about it. He had chosen not to believe those things, even though they might be true. And if they might be true, why couldn't he just as easily choose to believe them, to have faith in them, especially if that faith might lead to his salvation? Why not take the chance, if it might bring some peace, joy and love, and even forgiveness, to his life? Why not take the chance, if it would give him the strength to cope with his illness, to survive and see his sons grow up?

It was at this moment that Matthew decided to believe, or more accurately, to try to believe. He remembered the quote he'd just read from the Gospel of Mark: "Lord, I believe; help my unbelief!" The paradox suited him well. He decided to adopt that as his personal motto, at least for now. And perhaps someday he would adopt another motto: "God is my light." He looked at his Catholic University ring. A feeling of excitement, lightheartedness—even joy—descended on him. He was the prodigal son returning home to his father's love. He smiled and opened his Bible.

Made in the USA
Lexington, KY
20 May 2010